I0519717

SIGNALS FROM THE VOID

The characters depicted in these short stories are completely fictitious, and any similarities to actual events, locations or people, living or dead, are entirely coincidental.

No part of this publication may be reproduced, in whole or in part, without written permission from the publisher, except for brief quotations in reviews. For information regarding permissions please contact the publisher
Contact@RainstormPress.com

ISBN 10 – 061549269X
ISBN 13 – 978-0-615492-698

SIGNALS FROM THE VOID
Rainstorm Press http://www.RainstormPress.com
Copyright © 2011 by Rainstorm Press
All rights reserved

Interior design by –
THE MAD FORMATTER
www.TheMadFormatter.com

Cover illustration by R. Phillip Roberts
Contact by email: DollyMasterKingSouth@yahoo.com

DEDICATED TO
THE SETI INSTITUTE

THANK YOU FOR ALL OF YOUR
HARD WORK

ONE DOLLAR FROM EVERY SALE
WILL BE DONATED TO THE
SETI INSTITUTE

TABLE OF CONTENTS

Signals From The Void

FROM THE SKY, CAME THUNDER
BY R. M. COCHRAN

Click . . . click . . . , "Hiss . . ." static issued from the old radio George found in the attic. He was amazed at the antiquity of it, mesmerized by the series of tubes and transistors that warmed and seemingly ached from resistance once he plugged the machine into an outlet in the kitchen. Upon a bare board, not more than a foot long, components whistled and hummed, conjuring a yellow glow from the tubes. With a static buzz, the megaphone barked out white noise, hissed like an electrified snake and suddenly became quiet once he negotiated between the channels.

"I'll be," he stated, fidgeting with the numberless dial on the front.

As the radio warmed up, he smelled the components burn off the dust that had collected over the years, giving off a sweet odor of archaic books and smoldering hair. He giggled like a child, and rubbed his hands together, expectantly.

"If you can hear this. . ." More static emitted before George could manage to adjust the dial. "You're in grave danger. . . hiss. . ."

His brow raised and George hurriedly turned the knob again. Through the funnel that acted as a receiver, he heard the voice again, "Can you hear me?"

Reluctantly, he picked up a small microphone from a stand that had been mounted along the side of the radio, and pulled the trigger, "Yes, I can hear you." His hand shook.

"Good," the voice rattled. "What's the date?"

"December 19th," George answered.

"The year, what's the year?"

"Are you kidding me?" George had nearly laughed.

"Damn it! Tell me the year." Anger welled up in the voice, cracking through the amplifier.

"2112," George replied.

"Then I'm not too late." The voice had become calmer. "Now you must listen very carefully. You don't have much time."

"What are you talking about?"

"Damn it, human, listen!"

Human? George thought.

9

"You're going to need to do exactly what I say if you want to live."

"I don't know what kind of joke you're playing, Pal, but I'm in no mood for games right now."

"Your Mother was Teressa Newman, she died of old age in the very house you are in right now. You have three brothers, none of which made it to your Mother's funeral. You were born in 2080 in Grand Rapids, Michigan. . ."

"All right, so you know a bunch of bullshit about me, so what?" George mocked the voice.

"In 2.68 minutes, you will hear the sound of thunder in the distance," the voice lashed back, "That storm will mark the beginning of the end for humanity."

"Bullshit!"

"Just wait and listen," the voice remarked.

With a smirk, George waited.

Boom! Thunder clapped in the distance, reverberating through the building. George inhaled deeply from the sudden shock and adjusted himself in the kitchen chair. He stared at the radio on the table, cocking his head to the side before coming to his senses.

"Okay, I can see what's going on here," George laughed, "So you have instant weather broadcasting, so does everyone else on the planet."

"In 48 seconds, there will be another clap of thunder that will dislodge one of your Mother's antique cups from the shelf behind you and it will crash to the floor."

George squinted and turned in the chair, gazing upward to the shelf above the stove that housed his Mother's china. He smiled and began counting down from 48.

"3. . . 2. . . 1. . . "

Boom! Roar. . . The house quaked with a sudden jolt that rocked its very foundation. Crash!

George stood and wandered over to the broken tea cup scattered on the floor. He leaned over and picked up a fragment and held it in his hand. The sharp edge cut his palm and a droplet of blood glistened against the surface of the porcelain.

"And you will pick up a piece, thusly cutting your hand. It's from that drop of blood that we discovered who you are, where you were born, and what your destiny will be," the voice said, hissing slightly from the megaphone.

Clank. . . George dropped the shard, his face dumbstruck by the prophesy.

"Now will you listen?"

George wandered over to the table, beads of sweat formed on his brow, glistened like droplets of dew. He picked up the microphone and spoke, "Yes, I'm listening."

"Good, Mr. Newman," the voice cracked, "Humanity is very important to us, you're a part of our ancestry; primitive, yet necessary. We need you to survive."

"Why? What is this? What's gong to happen?"

"Calm yourself, Mr. Newman."

George wiped his forehead, a smear of blood smudged against his skin like paint against the surface of a canvas. His hands shook through nervousness and fear, sending the microphone from side to side as he tried to click the trigger to speak, "I'm fine now."

"Good. There is a bomb shelter in the basement of your house, Mr. Newman. It's behind a shelf. You'll need to disengage a clasp at the bottom to unlock it."

"Wait, what's going to happen? Why do I need a bomb shelter?"

Silence.

"Hello? Can you still hear me?"

"Yes, Mr. Newman, I can still hear you," the voice confirmed. "The thunder you are hearing is going to bring a storm unlike anything your planet has ever experienced. In two days, Earth will no longer be able to support life of any kind. Radiation will rain down from the skies and kill most of the lifeforms on the planet, wiping out vegetation, animal life and render the water supplies unusable."

"Radiation from what?"

"From a forgotten warhead that is due to explode," the voice warned, "It will cause a chain reaction of events that will be unstoppable, a series of situations that the governments of the world will not be able to remedy."

"My god. . ." George ran his hand along his face, "Will I be the only one left?"

"No, Mr. Newman," the voice seemed bothered by the question. "We are taking measures to ensure that there will be enough people to propagate."

"What do you mean, propagate?"

"As I said, we need your species to flourish. We need you as much as you need us."

"But. . ."

The voice, agitated and booming, cuts George off before he can finish. "You don't have time for explanations, Mr. Newman."

"Okay, yes, what do I need to do?" George asked.

"First, you will need food and water, enough to last for eighteen days. Do you copy?" the voice asked.

"Yes, eighteen days, I've got it."

"Next, make sure you outfit the shelter with enough odds and ends to pass your time until we can retrieve you," the voice stated, "You're going to be there for a while."

"The shelter will be enough to keep me safe?"

"Absolutely," the voice answered, "It was constructed out of concrete and steel with a thin lining of lead. You'll be more than safe, Mr. Newman, I assure you."

George sat dumbstruck, tapping his fingers upon the kitchen table, unable to bring himself to do anything else. He could feel nervousness well up inside his stomach, tying it in knots, making an acrid taste swell in his throat. Through the side window, he looked out into the fields that surrounded the small country home, watched as electrical flashes shot through the sky like phosphorescent spiderwebs, crisscrossing in every direction. The sight sent a shiver down his spine, surging along his limbs and finally resounded with a twitch at the tips of his toes.

"Mr. Newman, are you there?"

"Yes, I'm here." His voice was small and insignificant, drawing up images of a child, rather than that of a man. "I'm just. . . I just can't believe what you're telling me."

"Believe it, Mr. Newman. And believe that as soon as the Earths atmosphere is safe enough to enter, we will come to retrieve you," the voice reassured him, "But now you *must* prepare."

"Yes, right away," he jerked his head up and went to the basement.

Along the far wall, just behind his grandfather's workbench, he found the shelves that the voice had mentioned. He knew nothing about the old house, save for the fact that his grandparents had owned it for years until they passed away and left it to his mother. As far back as his memory would allow, George tried to recall visiting his grandparents home, but never had he entered the basement where his grandfather kept his workshop. He hadn't even been down here after his mother passed, there hadn't been the need.

He stared at the massive shelf which seemed to be more of a series of support beams rather than something to hold knickknacks. George searched the base of the unit and felt around the edges for anything that would indicate it could be moved. A protrusion, just behind the far rear panel, could be felt. He coursed his hand around, prodding the mechanism with his fingers until it finally released and pulled upward out of the floor. Its surface was gritty, caked with rust and age, making its movement stiff and labored.

He braced himself with his free hand and turned the handle until it creaked. The sound made him cringe, but George closed his eyes and suffered through the screech. With a gentle click, the door exposed itself as he inched the shelf away from the wall by only a foot. Grabbing the obstacle with both hands, he pulled it out just far enough to gain entry. A steel door greeted his gaze, bolted in the center by a massive beam that penetrated the frame. Hand over hand, he pulled the crank that fastened the mechanism in place.

With a whoosh of air, the door opened. George could smell age waft up out of the room, stagnant, putrid air that made him retreat a few steps before he could manage to step into the darkness. He felt about the wall and found a switch box at chest level, just a hands length from the edge of the doorway. Florescent lights buzzed overhead as he flicked on the switch, pulsing from their lack of use.

The furnishings were simple; a cot at the rear of the room, surrounded by several shelf units that held boxes of various sizes. George wiped away the residue off of one of the boxes, revealing its contents, "Beef stew," he muttered, remembering how his grandfather would try to get him to eat the stuff when he visited so many years ago. There was nothing worse than 'Meals Ready to Eat' and the fact they were prepared by the military didn't comfort him either. He remembered the conversations with his grandfather ending in him spitting the nasty stuff back into the bowl he was served, followed by a scowl and a lecture from his grandpa, "Food is food, I guess," he said aloud, staring at the boxes.

Along another wall, there sat a generator with its exhaust pipe protruding through the ceiling. George bent down and checked the propane tank at its side, "Innovative old bugger," he exclaimed, "A few years ahead of his time." He tapped the tank. A few more propane tanks were lined up against the wall like chess pieces neatly placed in order. Conduit ran from the generator and was attached to a set of outlets, fixed to the wall.

George clicked off the light switch and headed upstairs through the dank basement. He knew what he had to do, but still couldn't believe it. He was either very fortunate or completely doomed, he couldn't decide which. He closed the basement door behind him and sat in front of the radio to confirm that he had found the shelter.

* * *

"How long can I stay above ground?" George spoke into the transmitter.

"You have until the 20th at midnight," the voice replied, "Extinction will occur by the morning of December, 21st."

"Can I bring anyone with me?"

"No."

George took a deep breath. His mind fluttered with images of Armageddon, of angels and demons waging war upon the Earth in a final battle that would set the very ground ablaze. The simple fact that he was talking to something not of this world set his mind at ease as to the existence of angels. Still, it was a provocative thought.

"Will it be quick?"

"No. It will take six days before everything has died," the voice stated, "By that time, the radiation will begin to subside. Eighteen days after that, we can come to extract you."

"What makes me so special?"

"Fate."

"Fate?" George questioned.

"You have everything you will need to survive the end. Not everyone is so fortunate."

"Essentially, I'm just lucky."

"No. You're privileged. Luck is not a reality," the voice corrected.

"Can I say goodbye to a few people before I go?" George asked.

"Yes you may, but do not tell them what is going to happen. That information is not in their future," the voice warned, "But only as long as you have everything you will need."

"I have enough for an army down there," George answered.

* * *

Alice had only gone on a couple of dates with George, but had found him to be wonderful and kind. It was odd to find a man who could not only keep a conversation going, but opened the door for you when it was done. By no means was he perfect, but in such a small town, he was quite the catch.

She worked at the market in the deli section, throwing together selections of luncheon meat and varieties of cheeses that could be found in any grocery store. What the market lacked in variety, they made up for in service, and Alice prided herself on providing the most charm the store had to offer out of any of the people they employed. That is how she met, George.

He had been so shy that Alice was afraid he didn't like her. His awkward movements gave way to bursts of sweat that would make a bath towel cringe. But when she got to know him, his awkwardness subsided somewhat to reveal a well rounded man that would love her to the end of time. She couldn't have hoped for anything more.

When her cellphone rang, a burst of excitement shot through her, and lingered in her mind for a few minutes while she looked at the caller ID. It was George, right on cue.

Alice figured she would be cute and answer him by his proper name. "Hello, Mr. Newman," she said with a smile that was totally lost on the receiver.

"What?" George asked, taken aback by a sudden surge of fear.

"Um, hello George," she corrected.

"Oh, yeah, hi," he answered.

"Are you all right?" she asked, noticing an odd tone to his voice.

"Yeah, I'm fine, it's just. . ."

"What's wrong, Georgie?"

"Nothing, it's been a long night," he replied.

"Poor thing. Didn't get much sleep?"

"No, I'm afraid not."

There was a long pause as Alice waited for him to say more. "If you want to cancel our lunch date, I'll totally understand."

"No, I've been looking forward to it," he hesitated for a moment, "Can I pick you up a little early?"

"I don't see why not," she giggled.

"Great!" He caught himself. "I mean, I'll see you in a few minutes," he continued not wanting to seem too excited.

Before he left, George looked back at the radio and watched the tubes pulse with yellow light. He could have sworn it had winked at him as if it knew what he had planned. With his shoulders hunched, he sneaked out of the house and got into his car. He didn't want to think what would happen if the voice found out what he was about to do.

* * *

Her hair shimmered in the florescent light above the deli counter in such a way that it nearly brought tears to George's eyes. Alice was the only person he could think of when he found out the world was doomed, the only thing that he couldn't handle losing.

Alice flashed him a smile as he made his way up the produce isle, only glancing up for a moment while she prepared a pound of Black Forest ham for a lady at the counter. As he was about to speak, Alice extended her index finger, motioning for him to wait. She smiled at the customer and noticed George dabbing at his forehead with a handkerchief. She squinted and smiled again, handing the lady a package of luncheon meat.

"Georgie, what's wrong?" she asked, looking him up and down. "You look terrible."

"I'm so sorry for meeting you this way, but it's very important," he explained, "I have something to tell you." He looked around to make sure that no one was close enough to hear and asked, "Can you leave yet?"

Troubled, Alice turned. "Mike, I'll be back in an hour."

The butcher looked up briefly. "See you then," he said and continued carving a slab of meat.

From the Sky, Came Thunder

* * *

"You've got to be kidding me," Alice laughed, thinking George was playing a joke on her.

"When have I ever lied to you?" he asked.

It was true, George had always been straight with her, never so much as embellishing his weight on his Social Identification Card. A low hum issued above them, drowning out Alice's thoughts.

"Damn kids," George boomed over the sound of the Flier overhead. "They shouldn't be able to fly those things so close to the ground," he muttered.

Once the Flier had passed, Alice scrunched up her face in a look of disbelief. "But if the world is coming to an end, why hasn't the government made some type of announcement?"

"I told you, *they* don't know that it is going to happen," he explained, "It's one of those warheads from the 21st century. Hell, they probably don't even know that it still exists."

She shook her head in disagreement. "No, they were supposed to have dismantled them after the war with China."

"Governments have never been know to be honest, Alice. The name of the game is misinformation, that's what they do best," he replied.

"You've got to understand how hard it is for me to believe that an alien," she paused, ". . .an alien, George," she finally proclaimed.

"I know, I know," he said, "But it's the only information I have. How could they have known about all those things that happened before I even thought about doing them?"

"What do you think we should do?" she asked.

"I don't intend to survive alone." He took her hand in his own and said, "Alice, I think you're swell, and I can't imagine surviving the end of the world without you."

Alice blushed and smiled. "George, I think you're swell too, but the alien said that you were supposed to survive alone."

"I have a plan." A smirk spread across George's face.

* * *

"Is everything ready?" the voice asked.

"Yes, I have enough food and water stored to last for years, let alone, eighteen days," George said, "And I packed my reader and some other stuff to keep me occupied."

"Excellent, Mr. Newman," the voice cracked over the megaphone, "We only have a time line of about fifteen minutes to make a drop. When you receive the package, let us know."

"You're sending me something?"

"Yes, Mr. Newman," the voice explained, "But you are required not to open the package until the very last moment. If the container is tampered with, we will know, and you will not be extracted."

"But how will I know when it's time?" George questioned.

"We will send a recovery team to pick you up," the voice hissed through static as a crash of thunder boomed outside of the house. ". . .at that time we will tap on the door to you're shelter. Open the package and follow the directions. . . crack . . .hiss . . ."

"Wait, where are you going to drop the package?" panicked, George held the microphone to his mouth and tapped it on the edge of the table when he couldn't hear a response.

". . .in the back. . . yard. . .Newman. . .hiss," the voice cracked as the transmission moved in and out of frequency.

George stood on the back porch, watching the sky. Ominous black clouds rolled across the horizon, buckling in on one another, cracking with lightening that illuminated their surging forms.

"It's getting worse." Alice noticed from the doorway. "Will there be enough time?"

"I hope so." George jumped back as a bolt of lightening struck a tree at the far end of his property. "God, I hope so."

Dark clouds parted to a blue light, bellowing through to the bluest sky that George had ever seen. Ozone could be smelt in the air, mingling with the odor of wet dirt as rain began to pelt the Earth. The beam wavered and descended slowly to the ground, transporting the tiniest speck within its glow.

"There it is," he said pointing to the sky at a small box, twinkling in the distance. "See? I told you that they were real." George laughed, "Hurry, get downstairs, I'll be there in a minute."

Drenched to the bone, George made his way to the gleaming box that sat in the center of the yard. A volley of thunder smacked against the sky as he retrieved the package and ran back to the house. He wiped his face on a dishtowel and proceeded to dry the metal box. A set of four holes were indented into the surface of the container, spread out an inch apart and only a few centimeters deep. He played with the idea of opening the box, but thought twice before doing so, remembering what the voice had warned.

Descending the stairs to the basement, George fidgeted with the box in his hand. It was so light, almost weightless in his grasp. He wondered what he could possibly need for the aliens to pick him up.

"Is that it?" Alice questioned.

"Yeah, but what could be in it?"

"Maybe the aliens sent you some backup supplies in case they aren't able to get to you in time," she replied.

"No, that can't be it. They said to only open it once they knock on the door to the shelter," George rubbed his chin in thought. "I can't imagine what we would need. Maybe the aliens are hideous and they sent me blinders so I wont be able to look at them."

Alice laughed. "Yeah, I'm sure that's what it is."

". . .hiss. . .Mr. Newman, do you. . .have a copy?" they could hear the radio faintly from the basement.

"Shit!" George exclaimed and ran up the stairs to the kitchen, nearly tripping himself on the power cord to the radio as he fumbled to pick up the microphone. "Yes, I'm here."

"Did you receive the package?"

"Yes, I've already put it in the shelter," he replied.

"Good, Mr. Newman. It's beginning," the voice revealed as a massive bolt of lightening hit the tree in the backyard. "You must go to the shelter. We will extract you in eighteen days."

"Okay," George replied, "And, thank you."

"Don't thank us, Mr. Newman," the voice answered, "Thank fate."

A horrendous explosion shook the tiny house, knocking George to the ground.

"Hurry, Mr. Newman, it has begun," the voice warned.

"I'll take the radio with me to the basement," he replied, and extended his hand toward the plug in.

"No, there is no. . ." the megaphone cracked, ". . .need," hiss, "You will not be able to get reception in the basement," the voice replied franticly through the interference. "Go, Mr. Newman, before it is too late!"

The ground quaked beneath George's feet as he took the last few steps to the basement, throwing him to the floor. His head hit hard against the stairs as he tumbled, opening a gash on his forehead, right above his temple. He laid there in a haze for a few seconds trying to regain his bearings. Flashes of light spread across his vision before he finally passed out.

"Oh my god!" Alice exclaimed, "George, . . .George, are you okay?" she franticly shook him as blood gushed from his wound.

With adrenalin induced strength, Alice pulled George's prone body through the basement and into the shelter. She heaved him onto the cot, gently placing his arms at his side, and ran back to the shelter door. Several flashes of light penetrated the small basement windows as she looked out into the basement.

Franticly, Alice pulled the door closed as an intense flash of white light filled the basement. She fell on her back, tripping over the container as another quake rocked the house. Dazed, she scurried to her feet and bolted the lock on the door. She went to George's side and embraced his prone body. "Don't you die on me, Georgie, don't you die on me."

* * *

Through the night, Alice stayed by George's side, wiping his head with a scrap of cloth she tore from his shirt. With the contents of an old first aid kit that was fastened to the wall, she bandaged the gash on George's head as best as she could and prayed that he would recover.

As quakes continued to batter the little house, Alice watched over the man she loved, unable to do anything but watch as he laid there unresponsive. His breath was shallow and pained as his chest rose and collapsed sporadically. She wet his lips with her finger to keep them moist and paced the shelter when she found nothing else to do.

Alice slept on the floor next to George's cot and awoke every time the thunder jostled the house. She wept as George's body shook with convulsions. She screamed as his chest deflated with his final breath. She fell into a heap upon the floor when he finally died.

Over the next few days, George's body began to decay, to bloat and finally shrivel as his flesh made the transition into death. No matter what she put over her mouth, she couldn't shake the smell of rotting meat, of excrement that evacuated his bowels, of the sweet, rancid filth that dripped from George's corpse. Her eyes watered from the stench as his body blackened and deformed with decomposition. Every breath she took made her want to vomit, made her stomach lurch and recoil at the odor that seemed to cling to her skin.

Alice tore a scrap of fabric from her skirt and moistened it with some of the drinking water from the supply cabinet. When it dried on her face and began to let in the stench, she would wet it again and place it back over her mouth.

Her mourning turned to anger as she watched the body rot away into a pool of filth. She had come to hate George; for bringing her here, for dieing, for not letting her die along with the rest of the world. But, most of all, she had come to hate him for trapping her in with his remains.

As the days passed, she began to think that she would never get out of the shelter, that she would die from disease and starvation. Every time she ate, she would vomit. The stench wouldn't even allow her the peace of sleep. Her tired body exposed her to a type of insanity that she couldn't escape, an insanity that left her laughing on the floor, that made her want to rip at George's corpse, that made her wish she were dead too.

Alice forced herself to drink the water, to hydrate herself, but nothing more. Eventually, all that she could do was to stare at the body on the cot and condemn it for being so vile.

Finally, after eighteen days, just when she didn't think she could handle another moment in the shelter with the putrid remains of the body, there came a knock on the door. Hurriedly, Alice placed her fingers into the slots at the top of the container. With a release of pressure, the box opened. The top slid to the side to reveal a note which read: Alice, put on the radiation suit, we have come to extract you.

When she had put the suit on, the stench instantly went away. For the first time in days, she could actually breathe without revulsion. Through the narrow window on the mask, she watched the door as the lever began to move. She held the note in her hand and crumpled it before throwing it to the floor.

"They knew," she said, anger welling up inside her. "They fucking knew I would be stuck down here with that. . . that *thing*."

As the door opened, Alice flung herself at the obstruction, sending one of her rescuers to the floor.

Another form entered the doorway and grabbed Alice by her flailing arms. "I've got her," it said, the green slit it used as a mouth sneered as it overpowered the woman. "You were right, she has gone completely mad."

The other alien picked itself up from the floor and walked over to Alice. Within an inch of Alice's face, the alien snarled. "Good, you've still got some fight in you," its voice crackled and hissed, "you will do just fine."

Her arms pinned behind her back, Alice was escorted out of the shelter and up the stairs.

Out in the yard, Alice watched as a circular ship hovered above. All around the area, Alice could see hundreds of people being escorted to a large vessel, perched off in the distance, a few hundred yards away in a vacant field.

"Humans are so gullible," Alice's captor said.

"Yes they are," his comrade replied, "But they make wonderful fuel."

The other alien laughed, "Now maybe we will have enough to get out of this forsaken Galaxy."

All along the horizon, Alice watched as thousands of ships peppered the skyline, sending out tiny vessels that drifted toward the Earth, "They *knew*," she spat, "They fucking *knew*."

COFFEE
BY VOSS FOSTER

"Ma'am, please. The sign above the window clearly states 'class four pachyderms'. If you would take a little time to *read* through the registration papers given to you on your arrival into the station, you would see that you, like every other Mestacean, are classified as a class *nine* pachyderm." The human behind the window stared up into the dark eyes and sighed. "All class nine pachyderms are to report to the fourth floor, room four-eighty-nine, second window from the left. Thank you for choosing Earth as your travel destination." *Higher brain function my ass.* "Lorraine, I'm going on break. Take my window." Jim wandered back to the cramped, dark room and unpinned the badge from his chest. "Coffee."

"I wouldn't drink that coffee if I were you." A swath of graying red hair flipped around the back of a heavily duct taped armchair. "It's got to be a couple weeks old now."

The coffee splashed against the white Styrofoam cup. "I'll be damn pleased when coffee-drinking comes back in vogue. Maybe then we can get a fresh pot every once in a while." The thick nectar slashed across his tongue, twisting his face in disgust. "I just don't know how much longer I can drink this crap."

"Face it, Jim." Her eyes deepened from cobalt to navy as she rose up her own coffee cup. "We're fossils and coffee will *never* come back in vogue."

He snorted into the black liquid. "Maybe it'll be like lutefisk."

"Lutefisk?"

"In Scandinavia they have this dish called lutefisk and everyone hates it, but they all still get together and eat it out of tradition. Maybe the same thing'll happen with coffee."

She stood and drained the rest of her cup. "I wouldn't count on it." She coughed. "Have fun dealing with the Mestaceans. I heard a few of them talking about some illegal liquor, so keep an eye out."

"Why do the Mestaceans always come to Earth for their vacations?" She shrugged and walked out of the door. *Just to make my life hell.* Another mouthful of the too bitter brew swilled down his throat while he stared out of the porthole into the expanse of stars and planets. *It's a lot different from up here than down on Earth.*

"Jim." The voice vibrated from his earpiece. "We need you up on the second floor."

His muscles tightened. "Not Exotics."

"It's the new kid. He just got swarmed and we can't find him anywhere."

"Dougie, you know I hate Exotics." He drained his coffee anyway, already knowing he would lose the argument. "I worked up on the second floor for the first twenty years this station was open."

"It's either Exotics or the Mestaceans. Take your pick."

He tossed the cup in the trash and reattached for his badge. "What's in it for me?"

A groan passed over his earpiece. "Why can't you ever make this easy on me, Jim?"

"Look, if you can get us fresh damn coffee in the break room from now on, I'll get up there."

"Fine, but hurry."

Working out the cricks left in his neck from a night of too much work, Jim headed back out past the trumpeting Mestaceans, careful to avoid their wide, crushing feet, and wormed his way through the traffic jam on the stairs. "Please move, there's an emergency on the second floor." Just as the words left his lips, Jim realized his mistake. The Mestaceans on their way up to the fourth floor started trumpeting their elephantine calls, nearly deafening everyone else around to hear it. "Demons," he muttered, "Mestaceans are demons straight out of hell!"

When he reached the second floor landing, Jim found the problem right away and groaned – something was going on in room two-nineteen – ecosystem assignment. *This better damn be well worth fresh coffee.* He pushed open the door and fell right into the back of a particularly squishy Orvol. His face squelched out of the gel and, already sure he wouldn't like this reassignment, he crashed through the door to the back and went straight to the big closet off to the side, flinging open the door. "I figured as much." A very frazzled, frizzy-haired young man sat with his arms around his legs, staring at the floor. "Okay, kid, get up."

His eyes quivered as he shook his head. "No. No, no, no – I'm not going back out there. Those people are *insane!*"

"Well, those crazy people out there are the only thing standing between me and fresh coffee, so you're getting up."

Jim yanked on the kid's arm, but he stayed put. "They refuse to listen!" His voice was only just audible. "I had a Karzhian trying to tell me he had thick enough scales to visit Helsinki! No Karzhian can survive the cold weather in Finland!"

"Okay, I'll help you out this time, but you have to get out of the closet." He saw the youth's arms loosen from his knees just a touch and dragged him to his feet. Jim pushed him over to the window, "You're first problem is all this noise. You've got to get them to quiet down so you can concentrate."

"Excuse me." If Jim was a crier, he would have cried – the new guy didn't stand a chance and they both knew it. He raised his voice a little, "Could you please keep a little quieter?"

One or two people right next to the window turned to look at him, but they quickly dismissed whatever they may have heard. Grumbling, Jim pushed through the door into the body of the room. "People!" His voice banged around the walls, drawing everyone's attention to him. "Please keep your conversations quiet so we can process you as fast as possible!" The roaring speech died off almost immediately. "When your number is called *then* you may step forward." The look on the young man's face revealed his shock. "Don't worry, the voice will come. Now, just call the next number on the list and get a move on."

The kid grabbed the microphone and held it to his lips. "Number three."

I should have asked for more than coffee.

A Karzhian with thick, spiny scales padded to the window and handed over the number three ticket. "What is your destination?"

The reptilian alien tapped a claw onto the button of his translator. "I told you last time. I came to visit my mother in Helsinki."

"And I told you last time that your mother doesn't live in Finland. She would die from the cold!"

When he saw the Karzhian's face spike flare out, Jim took the wheel. "Can I see your paperwork, please?" He grabbed the stack of papers from the clawed hand and flipped straight to the second page. "Okay, everything looks in order, just head out to the shuttles. Thank you for visiting Earth."

With a final glare at the kid, the Karzhian walked out of the door and out of sight. "You just sent him off to his death, you know that?"

"Second page of the registration papers shows parentage. His mother came from the northernmost mountains on Karzhia, so she and her children can handle the cold. Call the next number."

With a downtrodden look on his face, the kid lifted up the microphone again. "Number four." The space in front of the window darkened with the ethereal form of a Murolite. The ticket floated up on a shadowy limb and landed on the other side of the window. "Can I see your registration paperwork?" The same limb floated over a clean stack of papers. The kid turned to look at Jim. "Why isn't he saying anything?"

"We haven't worked out a way to translate Murolite into basic English yet. It's too flowery."

"How am I supposed to find out where he's going?"

"She."

"What?"

"You keep saying he, but she's a she. Male Murolites solidify except during mating season, which doesn't come around until November."

He shook his head up at Jim. "Okay, how am I supposed to find out where *she's* going?"

"Second to last page of the paperwork."

He flipped to it and scanned down with his finger. "Phoenix, Arizona. Okay, just make sure to keep a spray bottle of water close by. If you ever find yourself feeling light-headed or dizzy just spray yourself down with the water." He handed back the registration papers. "Go to the shuttles and have a nice vacation. Number five."

Jim watched him process the next fifteen without issue. The kid even managed to send off a pregnant, molting Arechite without a hitch. When the room started to look less crowded he moved to the door, the hot coffee already in sight, but when he saw a new traveler come in he turned around. "Kid, forget those numbers. We need to get *him* processed first."

The bright yellow spider jumped up onto the counter, paperwork dragging behind it on a thin thread of silk, and raised a spindly leg to tap on his translator. "Listen," he said in a nasal voice, "I just need to get to Tokyo, so hurry up with the mumbo and the jumbo and get me on a shuttle."

"I still need to see your papers." The young man held out his hand, but the tarantula stared up with its shiny black eyes, unmoving. "Your registration paperwork?" It grumbled and flung the papers through the tiny slit on the bottom, biting through the webbing. Jim looked over the kid's shoulder, hoping he was wrong – his hopes fell through. "I'm sorry, sir, but there's an active ban on poisonous Thercanul on Earth and, according to this, you refused to have your venom disabled for the trip, so I can't let you go down to the surface."

"Kid, step back." Jim kept his eyes fixed on the Thercanul, waiting for the worst. "Just go push the red button in the closet."

"I think I can take a spider. We don't need to call security in for that little thing, no matter how violent he gets."

"Just push the button."

"I think you're overreacting."

Jim grunted and rushed back to the closet, slamming down the red button. The windows across the counter slammed shut with metal plates and the whole room shined with red, flashing lights. With a crash, a group of security robots came through the door, their sensor bars fixed on Jim and the kid. "We're about to have a situation," Jim said. A high-pitched whine filled the room, vibrating his bones. "That's the sound of a crying Thercanul baby." The robots don't need anything else to go on, rushing back through the door in a clean file. "You got put on a bad shift today, kid."

"Are you telling me that was just a baby?"

"Probably not older than three years."

He shook his head at Jim. "No. The book said full grown Thercanul are only just a bit bigger than that one."

"I told Dougie we needed to order new books, but did he listen? Of course not. Just trust me, that was a baby and the mom's probably not too far away."

"Jim!" His earpiece almost fell out with the force of the vibrations passing through it. "What the hell's going on up there?"

"We had a Thercanul that didn't consent to venom deactivation. A *baby* Thercanul."

Dougie sighed. "It's always you, Jim."

"The kid wasn't going to push the button. You should be thanking me." *And you should update the books.* "Look, what do you want me to do, Dougie? I can't control who comes in for what."

He sighed again. "Is security up there yet?"

"They're already on the move."

"Alright, just get the other travelers into the back room with you and take the emergency exit to the third floor. They're undermanned up in customs." The back of the closet slid down into the floor and the hallway behind it lit up. "And take the kid with you – he could use the experience."

"Do I still get my coffee?"

"Is this really the time for that, Jim?"

He refused to answer.

"Fine, you'll still get your damn coffee, just move!"

The vibrations fizzled out, leaving Jim's ear almost numb, and he moved toward the door. "Stay there." The door cracked open. "Everyone please follow me quickly. We have a bit of an issue, but we'll get you all processed as soon as possible." They all scurried toward him, looking behind them at the line of security robots. "Don't pay any attention to the security officers; just come back here, please!"

They all filed in and he led them through the hatch in the closet, "What about the Thercanul?"

"Kid, don't worry about it. Security has it under control, I'm sure. It's not the first time we've done this." *Believe me.* "Just follow me." He ducked through the doorway, the young man following behind him. "Okay people, there's a fork up ahead, you want to go to the right and the door should be open. They'll handle you in there. Sorry for the inconvenience." Once they all filed down the hall, Jim pressed on his microphone. "Dougie, I sent them over to room two-twenty-one, so open the hatch and have people ready to process them."

"You mean we're not going with them?"

"No, Dougie wants us both up in customs. Third floor, room three-eleven." He darted around a turn to double back. "I guess I still don't know your name, kid."

"Sid."

"I'm Jim." He twisted to the side to fit into the tiny stairwell. "So, how long've you been here, Sid?"

"About a week."

"Only a week?" He grabbed Sid by the shirt and dragged him to a crouch just as an Arechite whizzed overhead, squawking on about something. "Well, don't be too hard on yourself. It's almost my thirty year anniversary and I still see stuff in this place that throws me for a loop." They got to the hallway and Jim rushed along to a light. "Oh good, they're expecting us." He wandered in and said, "Sid, do you like coffee?"

"Like *what?*"

"Never mind." Jim looked at the room and only saw one very bedraggled worker taking on an army of vacationers. He sniffed the air, filling his lungs with an acrid scent, and walked up. "Take a break, would you? We'll get them all mowed down." She looked up at him with bags around her eyes and ran out of sight. "Sid, don't get too far from me – customs is the biggest hellhole on this whole station." *And I'm here with some kid.* "Okay, next!" The thick-skinned Karzhian from the second floor walked up and put two dark bottles on the table. Jim reached under the table and grabbed a small black box with one hand while he unscrewed the bottles. Tipping the first one carefully, he let a drop fall on the surface of the black box and nothing happened. "This one checks out." He repeated the process, but this time the box beeped a low tone. He flipped it over and read the screen and said, "Do you have any proof that you're allowed to transport Jelidal essence off-planet?" The Karzhian pulled out a pink slip of paper from one of his many pockets and held it out for Jim to read. "You're a pharmacist?" He slapped a label on the bottle in question, screwed the tops back on, and slid them across the table. "Everything checks out here and if you hurry you can probably still make the shuttle to Helsinki." The lizard swept out of sight. "Next."

A glowing Orvol wiggled over, its gelatinous body squeezing between the other people in line. "I don't know what kind of business this is, but I suggest you fire that young man." She held up a small mass of red goo. "He's trying to tell me that my son isn't allowed on the flight with me!"

Jim reached out a finger and poked the red mass. It squirmed and started to glow. "Alright, there shouldn't be any problem, but you'll need to get your son's registration paperwork verified which is on the first floor."

"He's only three months old!" More light poured from her body, casting the whole room in blue brightness. "I don't need to register him!"

Wonderful... someone else trying to tell me how to do my job. "Miss, all non-humanoid visitors to Earth need to be properly registered upon arrival into a space station despite age. You'll have to go to the first floor, room one-hundred-four and complete the registration process just like everyone else." A very noisy grumble came from the deep inside the Orvol, but she sloshed away all the same. "Next!"

* * *

A smile played at Jim's lips as he sipped what was sure to be his final cup of bad coffee. "Are you sure you don't want to try any of this, kid?" he said.

Sid sniffed at the outstretched cup and immediately recoiled into the chair. "I think I'll be fine."

"More for me." *Not that it's any good.* "So, you made it through your first week without killing anybody. Are you proud?"

He sighed. "Should I be?"

"I've seen a lot worse from some people. You just got caught in a couple of bad situations." He drained out his cup and walked over to the coffee maker. "Next time just don't hide in the closet." Tipping the pot as far forward as he could without the top flying open, Jim poured a few stray drops into the Styrofoam cup and chuckled. He tapped his microphone on. "Hey, Dougie."

"What do you need, Jim?"

"I'm on my last break up here in the third floor break room, but there's no coffee left."

Dougie groaned. "Is this really the most important thing I could be dealing with right now?"

"The faster you get some coffee in here, the faster you can get back to work."

"Fine," he said, "I'll have Judy bring some up, assuming you can wait that long."

"I'll do my best." The electric voice crackled out and, determined not to get drawn into any more work today, Jim tugged out his earpiece and stuffed it into his pocket just as the door opened. "Judy."

A short, slender woman sidled into the room with a white, metallic bag the size of her head clutched against her chest. The bag slumped down when it hit the counter. "Dougie said here's your damn coffee." She clicked her acid green nails against the stone surface and stared around the room with one eyebrow raised. "So, where do I make the coffee?"

Jim laughed. "Don't worry about it. Just go tell Dougie he really needs to update the reference books." Her heels clunked against the thin carpet while Jim sliced open the bag. "Smell this, Sid."

"I'll pass." Jim shrugged and filled the empty carafe with tap water to fill up the coffee maker. "So, you've been here for almost thirty years, right?"

"Just about." He clicked in the button and leaned against the counter to wait as the sound of percolation filled up the room. "I've got a few more months to go, but just about."

"How do you do it?"

"The truth?" Sid nodded and Jim grabbed another cup from the stack. Once the carafe got about half full he turned off the pot and filled up both cups, handing one to Sid. "Coffee."

A SMILE LIKE MANY VOICES
BY PATRICK SHAND

MAY

On the last day of school, Professor Darren State was alone in the classroom with Arnie, who had the unfortunate distinction of being the worst student in the entire class. Professor State, a young man himself, had found Arnie's scripts to be competent if a bit lazy, but that wasn't the issue—Arnie had stubbornly refused to do any of the quizzes given in class. When it was announced that there would be a quiz, he would sigh, scratch his greasy black hair, and promptly leave the classroom, leaving his classmates and Professor State quite puzzled.

"Arnie," Professor State said, trying to keep his tone steady. He knew that he was supposed to pay special attention to Arnie, so he didn't want to appear angry, but this was not the first time he'd tried to help the student. And really, State thought, the class was Screenwriting 101. It wasn't like Advanced Chemistry or a 300 level Math class. It was supposed to be fun.

"Yeah?" Arnie muttered, looking at his shoes.

"I have to submit final grades in an hour," State said. "Would you like to see yours?"

Arnie shrugged, but glanced down at the tiny printed numbers on the paper that State pushed in front of him.

56

"I'm bad at script writing," Arnie said.

State slid another paper in front of him. This was the cover of Arnie's final project, a twenty page script—there was a big red **85** on it. Arnie glanced at it, letting his eyes linger for a moment, and then looked away, whispering again, "I'm bad at script writing."

"You aren't, man," State said, suddenly feeling awful. Although Arnie's reason for not taking the quizzes had been "I didn't feel like it," State was beginning to wish he could just switch the 56 with the 85. 85 wasn't a *great* final grade, but it was passing. He shook his head, clearing his thoughts, then looked at Arnie. "Listen, I have blank copies of all four of the quizzes we took right here. That's all

33

you need. Your scripts were fine, you just need to pay more attention and do the class work. Here."

Professor State reached into his bag and pulled out a folder. He handed it to Arnie who, with a grimace on his red face, sat down. One by one, Arnie pulled the quizzes out of the folder, reading the questions, his expression twisting as he scanned the pages. Finally, just as he had every time Professor State had conducted a quiz, Arnie got up, put the quizzes down, and skulked out of the classroom, leaving State alone with a room full of empty, plastic chairs.

* * *

Professor State considered himself incredibly lucky. He'd only graduated college one year prior to being hired as a professor at Rockville University, and that was only because of the experience he had "in the field." In State's case, "the field" was essentially the act of annoying people on the internet. While he was a Film major at the college he'd attended, he made a habit of frequenting local film festivals and contacting the directors of his favorite pieces afterward. He would forward them copies of the latest drafts of the scripts he was working on, and in a few cases, said directors agreed to produce his piece. In other cases, they told him "Fuck off... and how did you get this e-mail address anyway, asshole?" but that's beside the point.

All in all, State knew that he was barely qualified to teach, but he thought he'd done a fairly decent job. For some reason, though, the thing with Arnie kept bugging him. State wondered if the kid could've passed if the class had been more fun, if he put in more work as a teacher.

State wanted to call his girlfriend. She had a way of clearing all of the negativity out of his mind with just a few words. She, however, had decided to visit her parents upstate during finals week, as she knew that State would be too busy to miss her. She'd only been gone for a few days, and he'd already discovered that she was wrong... he did miss her. He knew she'd answer if he called, and he knew she'd listen, but he didn't want to bother her while she was away.

He decided to go for a walk to clear his head. It was nice out, and he was done. Done with classes, done with grading, done with checking his mailbox on the seventh floor of the building with no elevator.

He'd been looking forward to this day for months. And it wasn't like he hadn't given Arnie a chance. He had. More than once. Arnie *chose* to fail. It was his own fault.

State walked out of his apartment and headed across the street to the preserves, a wooded area with a path for people to walk through to see the town's sorry excuses for wildlife. State wasn't sure why there needed to be an area reserved for people to check out squirrels, bugs, and that weird gang of geese that patrolled the tiny pond, but hey, it was a good place to run. After sunset it became the go to spot for the local kids to smoke weed and drink, but it was only 5PM, so State had time for a safe run. He was less afraid of running into drunk people than he was of finding himself in the awkward situation of running into a group of his students smoking up. He was young enough that they'd be more likely to ask him to join than to try to hide it, and State didn't know what he'd say if they offered.

He didn't have to worry, though, because he was alone with the squirrels and the hissing geese. Breaking into a jog, he couldn't help but focus on exactly the thought he was trying *not* to have.

He wondered what Arnie wanted to *do* in film. The guy was a film major, so he had to think he was good at something.

He wondered why he couldn't stop thinking about the greasy haired, lazy student just a damn moment.

He wondered why he cared so much.

He wondered if it'd be this way with every student he failed.

He wondered what the hell *that* was in front of him.

Something was glowing a bright, bright blue in the distance in front of him. The sun was still shining brightly, but the light he saw felt disconnected from that. It seemed to move like smoke.

"Hello?" he called, feeling silly. He jogged toward the strange glow, glad for a distraction from his thoughts. The closer he got, though, the farther the glow appeared to be. Confused, he stopped walking and, just as quickly as it appeared, the wispy glow blinked out of sight.

"Huh," State said, curious but not altogether intrigued. He lived on Long Island and had seen stranger things than a smoky light in the woods. Just the other day, he saw an elderly woman walking down the street wearing hooker boots, a tutu, and strap-on unicorn horn.

Deciding to head back to his apartment and catch up on his recorded television shows, he turned around and slammed right into a smiling girl. Stumbling back, State screamed and fell hard on his ass.

"Don't be scared," the girl said with a laugh.

"Whoa. Huh. I'm not. Not scared," State said, getting up and brushing his pants off. He heard a goose hiss in the distance. "Just... startled. I was startled. Whoa."

"Hello," she said, smiling widely.

State shook his head and looked at her. She was not at all dressed like she belonged in the preserves. She wore a sundress, long white gloves, very large, very thick glasses, and—oddly enough—no shoes.

"Hi," State said. "Um, are you lost?"

"No," the girl said, smiling. Her smile was so wide, stretching across her face like a worm unfolding to its true length on white pavement. Her voice was that of a little girl, but she appeared to be at least State's age, maybe older.

"Okay," State said, brushing his pants off again, even though he knew he was as clean as he was going to get. "Well. Sorry I bumped into you."

He tried to walk past her, but she held out a long, thin arm, blocking him. "Why?"

"Why what?" he said, realizing how uncomfortable he felt. Maybe he should have called his girlfriend. He missed her.

"Why are you sorry?" she said, reaching out and touching his stubbly face with her gloved hand. Even through her fingers felt warm, almost insubstantial on his skin. He jerked away from her, stepping back.

"Listen, are you okay?" he asked, looking down at her bare feet. Her clean bare feet on the dirty ground. Toes digging into the earth. "Where did you come from? Were you in an accident?"

"So many questions," she said. "So many Qs. Qs to be A-ed. So so curious, but not using your tools. So funny. So *curious*."

"...Okay, *wow* you're drunk," State said. "Do you want me to call anyone? Is there anyone..."

"Stop talking," the girl said. "Please. You're saying nothing. Absolutely nothing. Would you like to say something?"

"What the hell are you talking about?" State asked. He considered trying to run past her again, but he told himself that he wanted to help her, to see if he could get someone to take care of her. That's was his reasoning, but in truth, he was beginning to feel very, very afraid and he didn't know why.

"No Hell," the girl said, batting her big, blue, glowing eyes. "Never Hell. Now, tell me something."

State gulped. He didn't want to tell her anything, but he couldn't help it. Her fingers felt so warm and nice on his face. "My name is Darren State. I am a professor at Rockville University. I write. I love a girl named Carly and I think she loves me. I am twenty-four years old. I do not have a Master's degree, and I don't know if I can afford to go back to school. A student named Arnie failed my class, but he didn't have to. I—"

"Shhhhh," she said. "Shhhhh. Fine. That's good. You're almost saying something. You're almost there. Now, all you have to do now is listen. Do you want to listen?"

"I don't know," State said weakly.

"You'll have to be very careful," she said, holding up a finger and wagging it back and forth. "Sometimes you won't like what you hear."

State nodded. He felt pins and needles in his legs but found that he couldn't move. He wanted to take a step, just one step to shake the feeling away.

"Stop, stop, stop, it's okay," the girl said. "If you move, it'll ruin it. Now, I need you to close your eyes and trust me. Do you trust me? Do you? Good. Now, Darren State who teaches and loves and fails, please don't scream when I—"

* * *

Professor Darren State found himself curled up on his apartment floor with his cat, Liesel. She was purring, staring at his face with her green dinner plate eyes. State yawned, shook his head, and looked at the window. It was still light outside. Had he passed out? He vaguely remembered wanting to go for a run through the preserves, but for some reason his body felt completely warm.

"Weird day, Liesel," he said to his cat.

"Meow," she replied.

JUNE

When Carly returned from her cruise, Darren State took her to dinner at her favorite steak house. She wore a pretty dress and an even prettier smile. They'd been dating for a year, which wasn't very long, he supposed, but he felt like he'd been holding things back from her forever, out of fear that she would leave him if she knew how much he cared.

As she cut into her steak, State took a sip of water and, before he could stop himself, he said, perfectly casually, "Carly, I love you. A lot. I think you love me, too, but we're both scared of saying it for a whole bunch of weird reasons. But hey, here I am, saying it. I'll do it again. I love you, a lot, and I want you to move in with me."

Carly, her knife halfway through the steak, stared at State, her mouth a gaping hole of surprise. The hole then fell into a big smile, and she let out a laugh. State laughed too, and he couldn't believe that he wasn't worried about the fact that she found this funny, because *he* did too. What the hell had come over him?

"Wow," Carly said. "Wow wow wow wow. Okay. Well. Wow. You said that. That's a lot to say."

"Oh trust me, I know," State said. He felt his cheeks start to warm, and he imagined that his face was the same color as the center of his steak.

"Well," she said, stabbing a bit of meat with her fork. "I don't know what to say. I mean, yeah. Yeah, me too. I'm not going to say everything *you* said because I don't want to sound like a romance novel, but don't be surprised if I feel the same way about you and maybe sort of agree about the whole thing where we… you know, occupy a space… er, together. You know. For financial reasons only."

State smiled. "It makes fiscal sense."

They laughed and enjoyed their dinner together. State didn't know what had come over him, but it was almost as if there were a voice coming from inside of Carly that begged him to tell her everything, and he couldn't help but oblige.

JULY

Carly and Darren were asleep in their bed, curled into each other.

That evening, State had been working hard on revamping the syllabi for the classes he would be teaching that fall, so as he slept, his mind raced with assignments and quizzes and papers and films that he'd possibly screen. His dreams had been very vivid recently, and they always ended the same way. He found himself in front of a class full of students, all of them with Arnie's red face. They had different bodies—skinny girls, tall boys, every body type, each wearing different clothes—but they all had the same grimacing face, and they all walked out as soon as State wrote the word "QUIZ" on the blackboard.

He jolted awake in bed, his head pounding. Carly stirred next to him but remained asleep, her mouth slightly parted, her chest slowly rising and falling. Liesel, however, sat alert at the foot of the bed. She walked over to him, climbing carefully over Carly's outstretched legs, and nudged his hand with her head.

You woke me now pet me you smell weird pet me anyway, the cat said, rubbing her face into his palm.

State stared down at his cat and began to wonder if he was going crazy. He pulled her close to his chest, feeling her fur against her skin, listening to her purr, waiting for her to talk again. He finally fell asleep and, in the morning, he woke up to see Carly teasing the cat with a stuffed mouse on a string.

He shook his head and decided that he had to stop eating junk food so late.

AUGUST

When State walked into the apartment, he saw a decidedly miffed looking Carly sitting on the bed with Liesel in her lap. He looked at her, looked at the cat, and then shrugged.

"What did I do?" he asked.

"You told me you were gonna scoop the litter on the way out," she said. "When I came home, the house smelled like shit. You know that Liesel plays with her poop when the litter gets too full. You have to be more careful."

As Carly glared at him, State looked into her angry brown eyes and he began to hear something. It was soft at first, but it grew louder and louder the more he strained to listen. Though Carly's mouth was closed in a tight, irritated line, he heard her voice saying to him, *I love you I love you*

SEPTEMBER

It was only his second semester teaching at Rockville University, but Professor Darren State was feeling confident when he walked into Room 204, where he'd be teaching screenwriting to a room full of Film, Theatre, and English majors. He was more prepared than last semester; he had a better plan, better lecture ideas, and better films to screen. Everyone in the classroom would pass this time, for sure—even Arnie, who sat in the back with a blank, tired look on his face.

"Hello all," State said to a chorus of mixed replies. State walked around the room, placing a syllabus in front of each student, smiling at those he recognized from the Liberal Arts department.

"Hi Professor," Melissa Sherman said when he passed by her desk. As he walked away, he heard a voice—no, not *a* voice, *Melissa's* voice—say *My screenplay is about a girl who gets raped, but it doesn't specifically come out and say that she's been raped but she's traumatized and I based it off of my mother's life but I receive an eighty on the play because I'm not so good with the format of screenwriting, and I used the wrong "your" eight times. I resented that, that is what the professor takes from my script.*

Professor State turned to Melissa, his lip quivering. He tried to say something, but a squeak came out of his throat.

"Professor?" Melissa said.

"What did you say?" State asked.

"I said 'hi Professor,'" Melissa said, looking at the girl next to her uncomfortably.

State shook his head and moved on. His forehead began to prickle with sweat. He was sure that he was losing his mind.

He walked to the back of the classroom and, his hand shaking, slid a syllabus across Arnie's desk. Arnie looked at it, looked at Professor State, and then looked down, frowning. Professor State turned away, walking quickly back to his desk, but he heard... no, he *saw*

NAME	CLASSWORK	FINALSCRIPT	QUIZZES	GRADE
Arnie Canger	*65*	*80*	*0*	*48*

Professor State stared at his students, stared at Arnie, watched the students talking to each other, hearing them start to panic — they were looking at him, wondering what was going on. State put his hands over his ears, but he began to hear it all, all of it, so loud. He heard all of their script ideas at once, all of their final grades, all of their thoughts, all of their failures, all of what they thought of him, all of what they *didn't* learn, all of what they could have learned, all of it all of it all of it.

* * *

Carly was calling Professor State over and over, but State didn't want to answer. He didn't want to suddenly hear a bit of Carly's future — as nice as it was the last time he heard her thoughts, he knew that there was something wrong with him. He was hearing things that he wasn't supposed to hear. It had to be because he was stressed. Because he was worried about failing more students. He didn't want Arnie to fail again. That had to be it. His mind was giving life to his fears. That was it. That was logical.

In his dress shirt and slacks, State ran through the path in the preserves, his white tie flying behind his shoulder like a plane leaving a trail in the sky. He wanted to clear his thoughts, to stop the pounding in his head, but it got louder every time his foot hit the ground, every time, *pound, pound, pound.* A goose hissed as he passed the pond. As State ran away from the sounds, he closed his eyes, squeezing his lids shut, trying to push out the pain.

He wondered what he was hearing.

He wondered what would happen if he just concentrated, embraced it instead of running from it.

He wondered why so many students were writing so lazily and he wondered why he wasn't fixing that.

He wondered why his mind had chosen *now* to unhinge itself.

He wondered why it was suddenly so *warm.*

He opened his eyes and saw that he was surrounded by glowing blue light that moved like mist in front of him. It was warm, soft, like fingers through a glove.

"Hello," the mist said in a chorus of voices.

State sat down, because he found that his legs had gone tingly. There was nothing he could do but fall to his bottom. He felt something large hovering in the air above him, but he was too afraid to look. He knew the answers would be there, in the sky.

"Hi," State said weakly. "What's happening to me?"

A girl with big, circular blue eyes and a wide smile stretching across her face walked through the mist and approached him. "Hello again, you."

"I know you..." he replied, but he couldn't place *why* he recognized her. He felt himself looking through places in his memory, as if his mind were a hallway with many doors that led to different rooms.

"It is," she said. "Your mind, that is. But it's so much more than that. Would you like to open more doors? Would you like to *really* listen? You've been hearing a bit, but you haven't been *saying* much. No one here says much. You called us here with your little floaty machines and signals but now nobody wants to listen."

"Did you do this to me?" State said, and he suddenly realized that he didn't have enough energy to keep on sitting upright. He flattened his body against the ground, feeling the wet grass press into his shirt.

"A little," the girl said, bending down to him. "I can take it away, if you'd like. I can close your doors. I can keep you restrained, and you'll only think of me when you look at the sky. But I can keep on making you... *youier*. Or 'more you.' What's the word, professor? Do you want to teach people things? Do you want to hear?"

Professor Darren State found that he was mouthing a word over and over without making any sounds. He was mouthing the word, *yes*.

The last thing he saw before the flash of blue was a wide, wide smile descending on him, a smile like a worm, smile like the moon, a smile like many voices.

* * *

When Professor State opened his eyes, he expected to find himself curled up in Carly's arms with Liesel purring at the foot of their bed. But didn't hear purring — he heard hissing in the distance. And he didn't see his girlfriend or his cat or his bed — he saw Arnie standing over him, a lit joint in his hand.

"Oh Christ, you're alive," Arnie said. "Holy fuck. Thank God. Professor, can you hear me? Oh man…"

"Arnie?" State croaked, grabbing his student's hand and rising to his feet. "What are you doing out here?"

When he saw that Professor State was alright, Arnie shrugged, looked at the joint, and grinned. "What are *you* doing out here?"

"I… don't know," State said, racking his brain. He remembered going for a run. He remembered running past some fog. He remembered thinking he'd gone crazy. He wasn't so sure about that now.

"I think you fell down, man," Arnie said, leaning against a tree. His face was lit by the orange glow of the tip of his joint. Professor State looked at his feet, not wanting to watch his student smoking. It was inappropriate. It was wrong. Should he ask him to stop?

Arnie held out the joint to him.

"Want a hit?" he asked, and Professor State saw his student's lips stop moving, but sound and feeling and images burst forth from Arnie, flooded into State. He saw Arnie sitting at home in front of a blank computer screen, he felt his frustration, felt it in his fingers, he saw the quizzes that he, Professor State, had written through Arnie's eyes, and *damn* the sentences looked backwards, incomprehensible, mixed up. Wanting it to stop, wanting to put a halt to this flood of information, he looked right into Arnie's eyes and then all of the images and sounds died down and became one solid sequence of sounds, repeated over and over: *Talk to me talk to me.*

Professor State shook his head, declining the joint. He sat at the foot of the tree that Arnie was leaning against and cleared his throat.

"Would you like to talk, Arnie?"

* * *

Professor Darren State walked home. On the way back to his apartment, he heard the trees singing a ballad about the pending arrival of autumn. A squirrel ran past his feet, saying *Don't kill me don't kill me don't kill me.* He turned his doorknob, walked inside, and smiled at Carly, who smiled back, silently saying *I love you I love you I love you I love you.* Liesel rubbed against his legs, purring, saying *You are mine you are mine you are mine even though you are often stinky you are mine.* State kicked off his shoes, sat down at his desk, and began to look through his syllabus. He couldn't wait for tomorrow's class. He couldn't wait to hear what his students had to say.

SOMETHING IN THE ROAD
BY R. PHILLIP ROBERTS

For Raven Rachelle Dozier and Mr. Rod Serling.

"The time is now. The place is a small town in the middle of some-where. Anywhere. A non-descript tiny pinpoint on a map, like so many others just like it, spread out across the landscape upon a giant sphere of dirt. A mere speck of windblown sand amidst the vastness of space. Time. A rural outpost of civilized denizens. A community of decent average folk, all sharing similar needs and like-minded beliefs. All striving for a little slice of peace, happiness, and tranquility, to en-rich their simple domesticated lives. On the ever-elusive quest to ul-timate survival. Longevity of the species. Immortality. Living in fear of death and the unknown, much the same as you and I. The journey that lay before you could very well be your own. And in a moment, it will be, as we deposit you on the surface of the planet. Leave you in the capable hands of the town's only two peace officers. An invisible silent passenger, if you will, with a voyeuristic view from the back-seat. An astounding discovery is about to be made. A profound mys-tery unraveled. You are about to discover exactly what that some-thing in the road, might just mean, as we send you on your way. To another dimension. A realm of unbridled imagination. Infinite possi-bility. A little place we like to call, *The Twilight--*"

--schschschschschschschschschsch...

"Gosh, *dang-it!*" a man's voice says over the fuzzy distorted sound of dead air coming from the small set's single hidden speaker. "For cry-ing out loud!?! *That's one of my favorite episodes!*"

A hand belonging to the voice smacks the side of the portable television several times, in a futile attempt to bring the picture back. Another hand appears to turn the tuner dial, the former, now fussing with the coat hanger that serves as the sets reception antennae. With one final bang upon the side of its molded plastic shell, the hands cease fumbling with the controls. The power knob is pressed. The snowy image on the screen winks out, fading to a black empty void.

The abrupt silence becomes deafening. Then the man in the cell snorts, mumbles something unintelligible. The man on the cot lay facing the wall, his back to the other man who sits behind the desk, whose feet are propped atop its surface. The soles of his standard issue footwear obscure his face. Leaning forward, the man reaches for an object upon the desk, then brings it to his face. When he lowers his feet to the ground, his face comes into view, eyes now hidden behind a pair of dark tinted sunglasses, the lenses reflective like a mirror.

The man at the desk is Deputy Clarence Mervis and Old Man Tucker, town drunk and teller of tall tales, lay in the cell. The two men have been in each other's company since Tucker rear-ended Deputy Mervis' cruiser out in front of the jail with his pick-up truck hours earlier.

Deputy Mervis stands, walks over to the cell. "Oh well! It'll be light out soon, anyhow. I can get a better look at the damage you gone and done to my patrol car, you crazy old coot," the deputy says, smiling just a little. "Sheriff should be along anytime, now! Sure glad I'm not sitting in your shoes, old man! Sheriff's gonna be mighty angry at you this time!"

The man in the cell barely moves, merely grumbling but a few words. To the deputy, it sounds like one long muffled syllable of unintelligible noise, rather than actual words coming from another intelligent being.

"You sure aren't in no condition to be talking to Sheriff Hawkes right now," the deputy says adjusting the wide-brim hat on his head. "Shucks! Tell you what, old man! I'll keep the sheriff off your back awhile, so you can sleep it off a little more. Be back after bit," he tells the drunken man, before turning and heading toward the door that leads out onto the street. He turns the handle, opens the door, and steps out onto the concrete steps of the small government building. The dawn of a new day brightens the southern horizon, already ablaze with the suns' orange and yellow hues of blinding light.

* * *

Sunday morning. Bright and early. The streets are devoid of any other moving vehicles. No pedestrians are wandering about. It is a day of rest for all those who live within, or in the vicinity of this tiny rural town. Most are still in bed sleeping, while others are just waking up, preparing hearty breakfasts for those still slumbering away, all cozy under the covers within the comfort of their cool air-conditioned bedrooms. The place is virtually a ghost town, but for the one vehicle that slowly crawls along like some silent guardian on constant vigil. On a mission to protect and serve those who still remain behind closed doors, on what promises to be a perfect summer day.

The black and white police cruiser meanders its way through the downtown streets and enters the square. Sheriff Hawkes, the driver, pulls the cruiser up in front of the jailhouse, facing the front end of the deputy's vehicle. Immediately spotting Deputiy Mervis out on the walk, the sheriff wonders why the man has a worried look upon his face. But noticing Old Man Tucker's rusty old red pick-up truck sitting behind the other officer's cruiser, the sheriff has a pretty good idea.

Deputy Mervis approaches the vehicle before the sheriff even puts the car into park. The driver's side window rolls down. The deputy can see the sheriff's face, now, taking note of how several loose strands of long blonde hair hang down around the soft oval face. The sheriff wears sunglasses, too, much like the deputy's.

"Morning, Sheriff Hawkes," he says, leaning down to peer inside the car. Bringing his face within a foot of the driver's, he smiles.

"Morning, Clarence. Busy night?" Sheriff Marlowe Hawkes asks, with a tilt of her head inclined toward the other two vehicles.

The deputy lets out a small chuckle. "Guess you could say that, ma'am!"

"Anyone hurt?"

"Well, I'm not exactly sure about that, sheriff."

"Explain, deputy!" Sheriff Hawkes states with authority.

"Not so sure I can, ma'am!"

"Tucker inside?" she asks, bringing a hand up to cut the ignition.

"Wait! Maybe we best take a ride, first. Out to the old county road. I'll explain as best I can on the way," Deputy Mervis tells his superior. "And Tucker!?! That old man'll be sleeping awhile, yet. Tied a pretty good one on last evening, from the looks of it, sheriff."

"Climb in, then. We'll stop by Francine's and put the feedbag on along the way," Sheriff Hawkes suggests. "You can fill me in over some breakfast, then. Okay?"

"No can do, ma'am! It's Sunday! Frannie don't get things going until around noon, or so," he reminds Sheriff Hawkes.

"Right! Sorry, Clarence. One day just blends into the next around here, you know? I mean, look! Eli Tucker's drunken exploits is about the extent of any excitement we ever get to see around here."

"I reckon you're right, ma'am," he agrees nervously, lifting a hand to scratch behind one ear.

"What?"

"I'm not sure, really. Something that old coot was yammering on about, ma'am," Deputy Mervis says, then moves to the other side of the car and slides into the passenger seat.

"Sounds like you've got quite the tall tale to be telling me there, Clarence," she says, shifting the car into reverse and backing up.

"That I do, Sheriff! That I do!"

Sheriff Hawkes puts the cruiser into drive and pulls away from the curb. She glances to her left and notices the damage to the rear of Deputy Mervis' patrol car. Tucker's truck being the obvious cause, as it also suffers from severe damage to the front end. She shakes her head slowly from side to side. Sheriff Hawkes can only imagine what might have happened.

"I take it old Tucker's done gone and hit himself someone, then?"

"Would seem so," the deputy begins, "or some *thing*."

"I see! So, how far out we need to drive, Clarence?"

"Out by the old ruins," Deputy Mervis says nervously.

"Alrighty, then. Why don't you start filling me in on the details, Clarence," she suggests, trying not to lose her patience with the man. She likes Clarence, but every now and then, the man's lack of direct-ness frustrated her. Like now.

"Okay!" Clarence says, pausing to gather his thoughts on where to start. "Well, it was near upon two-thirty in the morning when I hear a loud crash out front. Startled me near to death, too, mind you!"

"I can imagine." Sheriff Hawkes interjects.

"I run outside to see what happened, and I find Old Man Tucker's done plowed his truck into the back of my patrol car. I rush over to see if the old coot's okay, and of course, the crazy fool's drunker than all tarnation, he is." Deputy Mervis pauses to swallow.

"And? What happened next?" Sheriff Hawkes asks, quickly losing patience with the man.

"He started rambling on about running something over. Said it wasn't like nothing he ever seen before. When he backed up to investigate, the wheels got stuck in the mud, over on the shoulder of the road. He tried to get out, but the wheels kept spinning. Finally, the tires caught and the truck lurched back up onto the road. Fearing he done hit someone, he grabbed his flashlight and exited the vehicle, to go and see what he done gone and hit. When he flashed the light on whatever it was he ran down, it scared the living daylights out of him and he headed straight for the station. And as you've seen for yourself, he rammed into my vehicle."

"Anything else, Clarence?"

"No, Sheriff! That's about it, I reckon!"

"Alright, I guess we'll find out soon enough, then," Sheriff Hawkes says, the thoughts of speculation now working their way into her head.

The two officers remain silent for the rest of the ride. Both have disturbing thoughts running rampant in their minds. Though, neither speaks of these things aloud, they both come to the same theory, or conclusion, and fear the impact it might have on their small community. And the rest of the world.

Nearly thirty minutes pass before they arrive at the ruins. Sheriff Hawkes and Deputy Mervis spot the body at precisely the same time. From a distance, it looks just like any other body one might see lying in the road at the scene of a fatal accident. So far, there appears to be nothing unusual about it. Both officers begin to fear that the old man might have actually killed someone. And more than likely, it was someone that both officers knew from the close-knit community that they were sworn to serve.

Sheriff Hawkes brings the cruiser to a stop and cuts the engine, keeping the car at a distance so as not to contaminate the potential crime scene. Both officers exit the vehicle and approach the body with caution. A heavy sense of apprehension and dread linger heavily in the hearts of each of the officers.

Neither can pry their eyes from the slain being, as they come to stand over the dead body. The victim is sprawled upon its back, arms and legs unnaturally bent and twisted. A head of closely-cropped sandy-colored hair is facing in the opposite direction. By its muscular tone, the body appears to be male. However, the large gaping wound in the chest makes it difficult to say for sure, without seeing the distinct features of the victim's face.

A long moment of eerie silence passes, as the officers stand over the corpse, letting it all sink in. Deputy Mervis is the first to look away and speak, "*Dang! Tucker done gone and made one hell of a mess now, wouldn't you say, sheriff?*"

"Yep. He sure has!" the female officer replies. She crouches down, careful not to kneel on the pavement and dirty the brown slacks of her uniform. The gold star pinned upon the left breast pocket of her light beige shirt glints in the morning sun. Sheriff Hawkes leans forward to get a closer look.

"What you make of it, Marlowe?"

Sheriff Hawkes chooses to ignore her deputy's indiscretion at using her first name, and takes a deep breath before answering. "Lookie, here!" She points to the gaping wound. "And then over here!" She points to a spot on the edge of the shoulder, approximately five feet away.

Clarence Mervis moves closer to stand next to the sheriff. Legs spread, hands perched upon his thighs, the man leans forward at the waist, looking more intently at the two spots indicated by his commanding officer. "Okay!?" he says, trying to make the connection.

"You said Tucker backed up and got stuck on the side of the road. Well, it looks like he was half right." She pauses, looking at her deputy's face, watching his mouth form into that stupid grin he always got, whenever the dawning of enlightenment struck his simple mind. Or when he got the answer right to a question on one of those game shows that he liked to watch on television so often.

"Sure did!" Deputy Mervis states.

"Well, look! If that congealing pool of blood and guts weren't all settled in like that, the wound would more closely resemble that rut over there," she explains, pointing at the muddy tire mark on the shoulder. "And look! See how the dirt and mud got thrown back like that? It's the same here with the blood, too!" Sheriff Hawkes points to the bloody trail fanning out across the blacktop, away from the wound. Small chunks of the man's insides lay splattered throughout the wet crimson stain, glistening under the bright sun, a host of flies buzzing about the slain carcass.

"Oh! So, you mean Tucker's wheels were a spinning?" Deputy

Mervis trails off.

"Yep! He got stuck in the mud, alright. But he must have run over the body again, not realizing it. The spinning wheel just up and ground this poor bastard's insides like so much ground beef, or something," Sheriff Hawkes declares. She stands and walks around to the other side of the body and sees the face for the first time. "*Dang*! If that isn't the *ugliest* thing I ever seen! Now that right there's enough to make *anyone* sick!"

"What?" Deputy Mervis asks, scurrying over to the sheriff's side. "*Oh! Dang, Sheriff!* You're close, but that right there's *beyond* any ugly *I* ever seen before! What in tarnation you think this here creature *is*, sheriff?"

Sheriff Marlowe Hawkes stares at the body a moment longer, then glances off in the direction of the ruins, located in the tall grass of the nearby field. The ancient circle of weathered monolithic columns are a mystery to everyone. Nowhere in the history books did it mention anything at all about them. The only knowledge concerning their origin, even what they were used for, all came in the form of legends. And some of those were so far-fetched, that no one really gave much thought to the outlandish theories, or fantastic tales handed down through generation upon generation.

"It sure isn't one of our own, Clarence! Look at them beady little eyes!" She points at the dead face staring lifelessly somewhere off to the side of the road.

"Maybe it's one of them there space aliens, sheriff!" the deputy says excitedly.

"It *ain't* no little green man, Clarence! *See*? Skin's same color and texture as yours, and mine. *Dang*! You been watching way too many of those science fiction stories on that telly."

"Then what you suppose it is?" The inquisitive deputy asks.

"Well, I suppose it very well *could* be alien, but not like the kind you got scurrying around inside that there head of yours," the sheriff says, pausing. "But I *also* reckon it might very well be one of our *own ancestors*, too! A missing link, like, in the history of our species."

"You mean, from the time before, sheriff?" Deputy Mervis enquires, referring to the time before known history. A time that had wrought great devastation upon the very planet, and must have taken centuries to recover from naturally. A time long before their very own species ever came into being. A time belonging to another race of beings. Distant alien cousins who had abandoned the doomed planet very long ago.

"That's *precisely* what I mean, Clarence!" she states, bending at the knees and crouching down once more. "We need to do something about this, before anyone else gets wind of it!"

"Sure thing, sheriff! You still hauling that old burlap tarp around in the back of your trunk?"

"Wait! I have a better idea." The sheriff begins to undo the lower buttons on her dress shirt.

"You mean--?" Deputy Mervis cuts himself short and crouches down beside the woman. "It would surely be wrong to do something like that, now *wouldn't it*?" he asks, but also begins unfastening the lower buttons of his own shirt.

"Think of the community. All those fine folks would just get in an uproar over something like this! Most of them been brought up to believing we're the *only* intelligent lifeform in all of outer space, *you know*?" The sheriff pulls the lower portion of her shirt open, exposing her belly.

Deputy Mervis does the same. "Well, when you put it that way, then I guess we're just doing our sworn duty, to protect and serve!"

Sheriff Hawkes grins. "I couldn't have said it better, myself, Clarence!"

The navels of both, Sheriff Hawkes, and Deputy Mervis, begin to open, enlarging to the size of a grapefruit. A series of pinkish tentacles slither their way out of the holes in each of their bellies, snaking their way toward the dead body of the humanoid man. On the ends of each tentacle are flat narrow pads lined with dozens of tiny suction cups. They find their way to different locations upon the carcass and begin to leach it of its nutrients. A natural acid secretes the fleshy meat within, breaking it down to a pulpy gelatinous substance that is sucked and slurped straight into each of the officer's stomachs.

Sheriff Hawkes looks over at Deputy Mervis, raising her hands to her face. "This is so much better than anything Frannie's got over at the diner! Wouldn't you agree, Clarence?" She removes the tinted eyewear, revealing two large bulbous eyes, severely bloodshot and twitching, throbbing all at once.

Deputy Mervis takes his own glasses off, exposing his bulbous, twitching eyes. He grins with delight. "Yeah, sheriff! You sure are right about that! Have you tried the brains, yet? You simply must, if you ain't done so, yet! They're quite simply." He pauses and lets out a healthy belch. "Ahhh... *to die for!*"

IN THIS TIME OF OUR DARKEST HOUR
BY R. PHILLIP ROBERTS

in loving memory of my beautiful friend Theresa Fairbairn

I remember the day the enemy first appeared to us. We were ill-prepared when they suddenly attacked, as everyone was first led to believe that they came in peace. But some of us gave it our all and fought back hard, right from the get-go. We put up quite a fight, too, despite the losses we suffered in our efforts to defeat them along the way. We even managed to put small dents in their defenses here and there, though our victories were always short-lived. Our enemy merely adapted, quickly reorganizing their entire network of death machines. And then they came back at us with a soulless vengeance.

Some of us managed to survive, making it this far on nothing more than the pure instinct to do so, with healthy doses of cunning and wit thrown in for good measure. The last four years have been a daily struggle for every precious moment of life we few survivors had once took for granted. Hanging on to the belief that we can take back what once belonged to us. Our home. A place now transformed into a nightmarish world of chaos and destruction. A world now overrun by the alien invaders who seem to be quite diligently intent on wiping out the entire human race. And those that are captured, taken alive, face an even worse fate than death.

To see those dying all around me and to still remain alive, living with the pain and anguish of it all. Clinging to the guilt. Taking each and every wasted life extremely personal. Each one just another stab in my already numb and broken heart. A slap in my weary and tired face. It is beyond the capabilities of most of us to even cope with. But I know that I must keep going and fight the enemy head-on. Face to face.

It is the only thing that gets me through each day. And the

next. The one following that. And so on. Until each day seems to blend into another, making it rather difficult to discern the details of one from the other. One gigantic blur of time that feels like an eternity of languid drawn-out seconds passing by in slow motion, and yet, it seems to move along as quickly as the snap of ones fingers at the same time.

It is hard to believe that so much time has passed, as it seems like only weeks have gone by since Dr. Humphrey and his rag-tag team of scientists fought side by side with myself and what few men remained of my unit. Along with those civilians who chose to join us, we hit the enemy fast and hard. We devised a plan of attack that looked promising in theory, but in the end did very little to cripple the infrastructure of the enemy forces. And so many lives perished, including Dr. Humphrey.

Jack and I had become very close over the course of the year-and-a-half we spent together. In our old lives, before the invaders arrived, I doubt that Dr. Humphrey and I would have ever become romantically involved. I suppose that in an apocalyptic world where one never knew if they would live to see another day, love becomes as vital a precious commodity as fresh drinking water, or food. I guess you could say that it was like sustenance for the soul.

In a world where we had both lost so much, even before the big invasion, we found solace in each other's arms. Holding onto one another through the night, or when we had the luxury to get any sleep at all, gave us a sense of there being something even more precious and personal to fight for. But as I look at things now, I believe it just might have been the catalyst to our downfall.

It was in the winter of '24, during that last battle for New Orleans, that we nearly lost everything. The facility we had been holding up in was attacked at dawn. The machines somehow discovered our location, due in part to our becoming too lax with confidence.

We had been pretty lucky up until that point, as there had

been very few casualties in the last dozen, or so raids that we had staged upon the alien assimilation factories. And I suppose that Jack and myself were in part to blame, as our personal relationship became a welcome distraction from the horrors taking place all around us. We simply were not paying as much attention to the details concerning our security as we once had been.

Losing Jack like that nearly did me in, as well. I was on the verge of a breakdown. I just wanted to lie down and cry myself to sleep. Hoping to never wake. Or maybe if I did, it would be to the familiar world I had known before, discovering that it had all been nothing more than a really bad nightmare.

But then I remembered something Jack had said to me one night after making love. As we lay in each other's arms and nearly on the brink of sleep, he leaned close to my ear. He told me that he loved me. And he added that if anything were to happen to him, that I must promise to be strong. To keep up the fight, until each and every one of those things was destroyed. That I must lead the charge in sending those alien bastards back to wherever they had come from. And so I did.

Despite what we had worked out before concerning our own world leaders' involvement in this invasion, be it solely staged by them, or otherwise, we did discover that there was indeed an alien race. It was a few weeks before I had made that promise to Jack, that the first one had been spotted by one of our team. And when he told us, of course we had to get a look for ourselves. We had to see what sort of cruel lifeform we were dealing with. Like they say, get to know thine enemy well, right?

As we hid among the abandoned buildings, smoke and ash making it a bit simpler for us to hide our presence, we saw the true identity of the alien intruder for the first time. It turned out not to be what we had expected, as it was not your typical Mr. Grey we had all been conditioned to think it would be, through films and science-fiction literature of the care-free world we were accustomed to.

Appearing only after the bio-mech death machines had

cleared the area out, the alien hovered above a pile of human bodies. And we soon realized that not all in that pile were dead. We heard the moans. The cries for help. We could even see movement within the pile, as those who were too badly injured, yet still clinging to the last remnants of life, attempted one last break for freedom. And we, watching from the shadows, were completely helpless to do anything about it. I for one will admit that I was too scared, even.

That creature was unlike anything imaginable. It was nearly the size of the mechs, which towered a good two stories themselves. Its skin was purplish, even shades of blue in some places. The head was like some giant insect's, sort of resembling that of a grasshopper, perhaps. And its body was massive. Round. Arms and legs were like the tentacles of an octopus, or squid. But the most horrific aspect of the whole scene playing out before our astonished eyes, assailing the already delicate fabric of our minds, was the fact that the thing began to randomly devour bodies from the mountainous pile. Bones and all. As if they were nothing more than some tasty snack in a party bowl free-for-all.

It was too much to handle and one of our number opened fire, the rest of us joining in. The ear-splitting sounds of automatic gunfire erupted from a dozen weapons nearly at once. All faces twisted into grimaces of anguish, hostile anger, toward the monster towering before us. But none of our shots met their intended target, for the alien being was surrounded by some sort of force field. We could see its spherical shape as the bullets struck the semi-invisible shield. And when all of our weapons clicked on empty, we ran away from the area, our collected fear of the menacing creature driving us to push ourselves even harder in our efforts to outrun whatever horror that thing might send after us.

This new knowledge only made us stronger in our determination to find a way to turn these invaders away. Take back our lives. Our very existence. And this led to our decision to find a new place to hold up in. A place outside the city where we could continue our research on the mechs, in order to gain a different perspective on how to best fight them.

On the day we were set to depart is when the mechs caught us by surprise, hitting us just before dawn. The building was coming down around us, as we scattered and took cover. Some of us were able to don our gas masks and other protective gear before the lethal gases began seeping in. Those caught unprepared became infected with the poison. Many died immediately, while others simply lost their minds and turned on their comrades.

I spotted Jack as he tried to make his way toward the emergency exit, where myself and several others were gathering to depart. Then it happened. A steel rafter beam dislodged and came crashing down on him, crushing the doctor instantly. And I screamed as I ran toward the spot where Jack's lifeless body lay, no longer caring about the danger that I was in. More of the building came tumbling down. I was pinned to the ground and unable to feel my legs. Nor could I move them.

I almost lost my own life in those last moments. And would have, too, if not for a brave young man who pulled my broken body from out of the rubble. He picked me up and slung me over his shoulders, carrying me to relative safety, right before the whole place was blown to smithereens. I lost consciousness at some point and do not remember anything that happened until the moment I once again opened my eyes.

To my dismay, I found that I had lost the use of both my legs. Without proper medical attention they soon became infected and had to be removed above the knees. And thus I became confined to a wheelchair. Not exactly the type of existence for a soldier when the entire world was on the brink of destruction. The entire human race on the verge of extinction.

No longer able to stand and fight off the invading forces, I opted to go into the desert with some of the scientists and researchers that had worked closely with Dr. Humphrey. I figured if I were no longer able to combat my enemy directly, than I was surely going to have to find another way. So we headed west to a little known secret facility somewhere deep in the open desert. Underground, actually. And aren't they all?

The place had everything we needed from research labs to medical supplies. The place even had hot running water, thanks to the place being completely self-sustainable due largely to the intense rays of the Nevada desert sun energizing the strategically placed solar panels across the desert floor.

As well, a full staff of various personnel were already in place when we arrived. This included a small military faction made up of various soldiers. Men and women who had survived the initial onslaught of the attack and managed to find their way to the facility, in hopes of finding others who could fight. Reasons not so very different from my own.

In those slightly less than few years, I devised a plan. One that I kept to myself for awhile, at least until we could learn more about the bio-mechs. And this was made easier by the fact that there were already half a dozen specimens being studied by the scientists at the facility. All I needed to do was study the details of the information already obtained. Before too long, I joined one of the research teams and got a little hands-on experience myself. I became obsessed with wanting to know every little detail concerning the intimidating war machines. And it paid off, too.

Once I felt confident that my plan would work, I began to talk more openly about it with the others. At first they thought I was crazy. But I soon won them over. As I said to them, we have no other options remaining to us. That my plan was the only thing that made any sense, considering how every single time we tried to use conventional means against our enemy, we got our asses handed to us. And at that rate, there would come a day when there would be no one left to stand and fight. Cold hard facts to which everyone agreed.

Once everything was in place, we were ready to begin.

However, we still needed five more volunteers, myself being the first. Thinking this vital detail would go over like a lead balloon, I was surprised to find that more participants than were required were more than ready to make the sacrifice that I was asking of them. And thus began a long and painful journey that the six of us could never return from. All in the name of mankind's salvation.

I can only speak for myself, though I am quite sure the experience was much the same for the others, for we each endured the same series of operational procedures. The first of many to follow being the removal of the lower extremities, leaving each of us with nothing below the hips, as this would allow what was left to be inserted properly into the cavities of the mechs.

My memory is hazy at best, what with all the painkillers and states of unconsciousness along the way. But I do recall that once the healing process was complete, I found that I was now fused to the inner workings of the machine body. What followed was the most excruciatingly long process of assimilation, as each of us underwent the intricate hardwiring into the sophisticated machines' computer terminals.

For each series of hookups, the doctors peeled back the layers of skin, exposing the raw sinewy muscle below the surface. Every nerve ending felt like it was on fire, even though the meds were the strongest we had available. But my determination, and I suppose the trained warrior within myself, carried me through. It gave me the willpower to withstand the entire year-long transformation. And only one of our numbers did not make it, leaving us with only five fully-functional bio-mechs. Only now we were in control of the mechanical monsters.

We trained for several weeks, learning how to control our new body parts, so to speak. It was a good thing, too, for the enemy began to close in on our location a few days ago. And we are prepared to fight like never before.

For the record, Jack never destroyed Carol's notes like he led Dr. Davis to believe. He gave them to me, knowing full well that

I would see that they got put to good use in deciphering the alien code. It has become useful in the assimilation process, as the five of us are now able to communicate directly with the hive, including the Mothership hovering in space near our co-ordinates. This is how we know that they are on their way to seek us out. Destroy us.

We prepare to depart shortly. Right after I finish this recording. But in case I never get the opportunity to make another, I want it to be known that I have made this ultimate sacrifice for the last remnants of humanity. I will keep fighting for our survival. No matter what it takes.

They are crossing the desert. Getting nearer every second. But we are ready for them this time. And as we prepare to depart and meet them out in the open, I confess that I not only do this in the name of freedom, but for the loss of Jack, too. A man that I now realize I loved with all of my heart.

Major Terri Lynn Fairchild
USMC - Special Ops
Audio Log Date: 09-11-2027

* * *

The dark shape rose out of the tall grass like a giant scarecrow, or even like that of a very large yard gnome, its dull metallic body gleaming in place as the sun began to rise in the east. But the approaching figure knew exactly what it was. Had seen plenty of them during the invasion years. The ultimate battle between man and machine that had lasted nearly a decade, until one side had been defeated altogether. Completely wiped out as if they had never existed, but for the constant little reminders found here and there in the stark and barren landscape. Relics of another time, slowly being devoured into the Earth as she slowly recovered from her wounds.

Rust had set in on the ancient machine, especially in places where it looked to have suffered damage in some long ago battle. Dented in places and broken in others, the metal goliath stood silent and immobile under the early morning light, with the brilliant sun on the horizon offering the promise of a bright sunny day. Not a cloud could be seen in the ever-brightening blue ether. A far cry from what the sky had once looked like when the mechs had waged war upon the entire population of the planet.

Curious, the figure moves closer to the hulking beast, no longer the menacing war machine it had once been before coming to its final resting place. No longer able to function in its current death-like stasis. Harmless. Nothing more than a towering heap of scrap metal. But being somewhat of a history buff, the stranger hopes to find the memory drive intact, and begins to climb the old decaying monster.

On closer inspection, the thing looks to be more damaged than at first thought to be. Upon reaching the breastplate and tinted glass shield, the stranger easily peers inside a large-sized hole that had nearly shattered the entire plate of protective glass. The empty sockets of a human skull peer back from within, the skeletal remains of the machine's biological counterpart bleached from the many years of exposure to the elements.

It might have frightened the stranger, even sent a shiver up the old spine, if indeed those human emotions, reactions, could even be felt by the cloaked figure. Reaching an arm inside, the mysterious drifter soon finds what it is looking for and releases the device from its connection to the mech's digital relay board, before descending back down to the ground.

Reaching inside its cloak, the stranger pulls out a cable and attaches it to the hard drive. Satisfied when the thing works, the figure smiles and places the device inside an inner pocket. And while the information is processing, the stranger casts another glance up at the towering machine, the hood of the cloak falling back to reveal the metallic shiny surface of the artificial being's face. What passes for the robot's eyes glow red like two tiny dots of LED lights.

Letting out what passes for a sigh, the robot turns back in the direction it had originally been heading and continues on its journey. The last recorded message from the bio-mech plays out in its digital brain. And for the first time in its long and endless life, the robot experiences what he believes sadness might have once felt like to a human being. And by the time the message comes to an end, feels a knot in the place its heart would be if the robot drifter indeed had one.

TRI-COPIER 6000XT
BY FRANCES PAULI

"What the heck is that?" Dylan Lowwater closed the door to the Alien-Human Relations department with a dull thud. He rolled his eyes and looked around the room, as if the noise, the door itself, enacted a personal assault on his senses. It all spelled one thing in his book: boredom.

"It's the mail, man," the new kid answered from behind the desk. He gave the item in question a sharp thump with one, grubby finger. "I heard they offered you a transfer."

"Yeah." Dylan crossed the room and shooed the kid out of his spot. He deposited his brown-bag lunch on the slick surface. "This isn't even ours." He squinted at the square package and short stack of envelopes also occupying the desktop. They currently blocked his favorite place to take a nap. "It's off by two floors, moron. Didn't you check it?"

The new kid just shrugged and grabbed a stack of printouts from the department's newest acquisition: a Tri-copier 6000XT. He flashed one of the papers in Dylan's direction--a three-dimensional shot of the kid's hand flipping him the bird. "Why didn't you take it?" he asked.

"Take what?"

"The promotion, the transfer." He waved a hand to indicate their surroundings. "A chance to skip out on the shit shift here."

"I like the shit shift," Dylan stated dryly. "And that's a flagrant abuse of company property, dipshit." The transfer offer had only come through two days ago, but news traveled fast on the station, faster than the mail at least.

"Like you haven't done it." The smartass kid sneered and tucked his tri-photos under one scrawny arm. He reached the door and then tossed back over his shoulder. "What's to like about working in the middle of the freaking night?"

"Peace and quiet, man," Dylan answered. Of course he'd done it. The tri-copy of his genitals in full, three-dimensional glory was one of his prized possessions, but the new hire could use to learn a little respect. "Peace and freaking quiet." He kicked back in the chair and waited for the kid to leave. When the door thumped closed, Dylan leaned forward and gave Medical's mail a lethargic once-over.

They made a point of hiring idiots in the mailroom. They had to. He couldn't come up with a better explanation for why the post always went awry, why they got Medical's mail twice a week and theirs hadn't been delivered to the right department in months. One time he'd had to trek all the way to the communications relay to fetch it. The walk had eased the drudgery though. He should call around and see where theirs had landed tonight. He should have asked for a transfer to the mail room.

He chuckled and slid the square package--smaller than a breadbox, plain brown wrapper--to the side, then sifted through the envelopes. "Junk, junk, crap, hello?" The magazine slid out of its celowrapper without any signs of tampering. The glossy cover read: *Galaxy Girl.* "That's more like it." Dylan nodded. "Alien booty."

He fanned through the pages, one eyebrow cocked and an ear open for any late night applicants. There wouldn't be any. They never had any business down here on his shift. He considered it one of the job's perks. Still, he reached into the desk drawer with his free hand and slid out a drug testing packet. One time, he'd had a late night visitor. Even though the pregnant Ursine hadn't crawled across his carpet looking for a drug test, she'd taught him one thing quite clearly. You never knew *what* might come through your door.

Dylan nodded appreciatively at page seven and kept flipping. When he reached the center staples of the spine, he paused. "Nice eyes," he said. "Very nice." The flap opened, spilling over the magazines borders like a glossy flag. "Egh! Agh," He gasped, slammed the paper shut and shoved the magazine back to the desk with a shudder. "Holy crap."

That was the problem with an intergalactic society, he decided. You never knew what you'd find under somebody's clothing either. He shivered once, then shrugged and pushed the mail back into a rough stack. He reached for the package instead and...missed. Dylan squinted at the box. He could have sworn he'd set it down closer than that. "You're losing your mind, man."

He lifted it gingerly, placed it back on top of *Galaxy Girl,* and turned to the wrinkled brown paper bag containing his usual peanut butter sandwich. He'd abandoned all experiments in exotic cuisine years ago. Peanut butter suited him fine. It was boring, yeah, but he took comfort in that. In light of that centerfold, boring didn't seem so bad.

He took his first bite, chewed mechanically and swallowed the remaining lump. The sandwich had just reached his mouth again when he heard the distinct bump of cardboard box against tabletop. He froze mid-bite.

"What the?" Dylan lifted his attention and his lips from the sandwich. The square package had shifted position. It sat, as if innocent, beside the pile of mail. He put the sandwich down, laying it carefully on the paper bag, and reached toward the box. Before his fingers made contact, however, the package rocked sharply back and forth.

"Mother of Christ!" He jumped on reflex, ending up plastered against the wall behind his desk and eyeing the suspicious box across his overturned chair. He could hear a distinct squishing noise as the package shifted, slowly, another two inches away from the rest of the mail. *Something* was alive inside the cardboard, and Dylan could imagine a long list of what that something might be. He wanted absolutely nothing to do with any of the possibilities.

He sidled around the edge of the room, watching the cardboard cube's progress with his full attention. By the time he passed the station's ID poster and slammed the call button, the thing teetered on the edge of the desktop. Dylan watched it waver at the lip, flirting with the station's artificial gravity.

"Security." The bored voice rang through the comm.

"I need medical down here immediately!" Dylan squealed as the box dropped. It hit the floor and he did his best to merge with the wall at his back.

"Are you having a medical emergency?" Now the bastard sounded hopeful.

"Not exactly." Was it an emergency? Dylan leaned away from the wall and assessed his situation. The package sat, unmoving, on the carpet by the desk leg. He thought fast. They already thought he was an idiot in security. The Ursine incident had played hell with his reputation. If he called in a false alarm now, he could kiss any hope of a social life goodbye. He took a deep breath and let his initial panic settle. "We have their mail."

"Right."

"Just get them down here." Dylan sighed. He lifted his finger from the button and leaned one elbow against the wall. He cocked his head. He watched the package on the carpet and waited.

Nothing happened. Dylan straightened and cleared his throat. He took a tentative step toward the desk. The station poster scrolled its call letters across the wall beside him. He took another step, leaned over and gave the box a good long stare. The package failed to move.

He squatted and reached one finger toward the cardboard. He pushed it. He tapped quickly on the top and then flipped it onto its side. It should have been heavier, much heavier. It definitely shouldn't have had a sticky, gaping hole the size of his fist on the bottom.

"Crap," he said. The bottom of the box was melted or burned or who the hell knew what. More significantly, Dylan felt, the box was now empty. He stood up rapidly. "Crap, crap."

He sat on the desk's edge and crossed his arms. He drew his brows together and tried to stare a second hole in the box. Whatever had been shipped in that package moved of its own accord and had no trouble decimating a layer of sturdy cardboard. It had also escaped into Dylan's work/nap space. "Great," he growled. "Freakin gre-aaaah!"

Something touched his foot. He looked down in time to see one thick, pink tentacle disappear into his pants leg. Dylan could feel the soft pressure of *it* climbing his leg.

"AAAAGGGH!" He shouted and jumped up. His hip slammed into the desk, knocking the stack of mail in a landslide across the floor. Dylan hopped across the room with one hand working at his zipper. He shook his leg, but the warm, wet pressure continued to climb over his knee.

He opened his pants and reached down the leg, shaking the cloth wildly. The damned thing clung on, sticking to his skin like glue. Dylan writhed and shook and shimmied, and the creature in his pants didn't budge.

The door chimed. He froze and lifted his eyes slowly to the room's entrance. A woman stood inside the open doorway. She wore the frock uniform of a Medical employee and a horrified expression. *Thank god*, he thought.

He stumbled toward her a step. "Help. Your mail."

The woman's dark eyes dropped pointedly toward his waist and to his arm jammed up to its elbow into his pants. She scanned forward, and rested her gaze for a split second on the glossy magazine lying on the room's carpet. The girlie rag had landed open. The centerfold flapped slightly in the currents of the department's air circulation system. "No!" Dylan shook his head. It looked bad. Of course it did, but he didn't deserve that look.

"You're sick," the girl announced. Her face twisted into a grimace of disgust. She spun on one sharp heel, turning her back to him and stepping back through the doorway, without her mail.

"Wait!" Dylan screamed. He took a half step forward, his lowered pants hindering the movement. As he did, his reaching fingers came into contact with something soft, warm, and slightly slimy. His hand twitched away from it, but a sharp electric sting exploded through his arm and up into his shoulder. "Shi…" His knees buckled and he fell forward. He crumpled to the carpet, felt a wave of nausea wash through his innards and heard the staccato click of the mail girl's heels in the hall outside. She abandoned him to his fate. The last thing he heard as blackness took him was the dull thud of the door.

* * *

His head hurt. He opened his eyes and tried to shake away the bleariness. The room had tilted. Dylan could see the legs of the desk and the fat lint wads and paper bombs that lived under it. A light flashed across the scene. It made the pain in his head throb harder. His own moan sounded feeble and far away. What the hell had happened? He'd fallen down. That much was apparent. He was lying on the floor and most likely dying. Dylan tried to think. The pain in his head receded a little. He should remember something.

There was a poisonous alien in his pants.

The light flashed again, accompanied by a mechanical hum. He tried to move, but the right side of his body was paralyzed. He wiggled his fingers. *Not paralyzed--arm still in pant leg.* He groaned and rolled over, extracting his arm from his clothing. His fingers ached, but he quickly deduced that he was, quite probably, not dying. The light flashed again.

"What the hell?" He rolled to his knees, feeling along the fabric of his pants for stowaways. "Nothing." Whatever stung him senseless no longer resided in his trousers. Good news. He exhaled a breath that was only half relieved. "Great, it's loose again." The light flashed. This time, he recognized the noise. "Tri-copier 6000XT."

He scooted backwards until he could brace his torso against the wall and then attempted to fix his pants. The tri-copier flashed twice more before he managed to get himself properly dressed. Once he was zipped again, he stole a cautious peek around the corner of the desk.

The Tri-copier 6000XT stood at the far side of the office. The lid panel hovered slightly ajar. Dylan shivered. A fat pink tentacle hung over the lip of the copy surface. As he watched, it contracted once and slowly pulled itself up under the heavy lid. The light flashed, the mechanism hummed and a thin tri-D copy slid out of the slot and onto the receptacle tray.

"I'll be damned," Dylan whispered. He scanned the room for a weapon, but nothing useful presented itself. The copier continued to flash and spit out images of whatever horror Medical had mail ordered. "Shit." He slid around the desk, crawled out into the open and shuffled on hands and knees toward the hulking contraption. His eyes focused on the rectangular control panel. They'd only had the thing installed a few weeks ago. He let his gaze slide to the back of the machine. "Model 6000XT with built in shredder attachment." He'd read the brochure during a bout of boredom. A shredder attachment, he'd thought, what had that little gadget added to the cost? He'd imagined the salesmen's glee when he'd saddled them with the useless add-on. He wished the bastard was here now so he could thank him.

His hand hit something slick and slid out from under him. He sprawled on his belly, one cheek pressed against the cool pages of the offensive *Galaxy Girl.* Keeping his eyes on the copier, Dylan pushed up to his knees. He reached down and rolled the magazine into a tight tube. Hell, it was better than nothing. The machine flashed and spit out another copy. He crawled forward again. The unit's lid wobbled slightly, but remained closed on the creature. Did it have a clue what it was doing? He imagined it just happened to crawl onto the copier, that the device's auto copy had triggered at the accidental brush of a tentacle. He hoped it had. Dylan didn't relish the idea of sending a sentient being through the shredder, but this little blob had knocked him unconscious with one sting. It had invaded his personal space, made him look like a pervert, and greatly reduced the number of work hours he'd have left to spend napping. The damned thing had to go.

He watched the copier lid, as if it might release the tentacled devil at any second. He'd have to open it. His teeth clenched briefly at the thought. He'd have to lift the lid and smack the thing just right to knock it in. Bravery had never been his strong point. He swallowed a lump of nerves and crawled closer. His fingers twitched at the memory of the tentacle's sting. The copier flashed out another print.

When he shifted into a crouch, the lid moved. Dylan froze, teetering on his toes, one hand clutching a girlie magazine and the other against the carpet, steadying, balancing. He held his breath. The machine hummed and copied another image. He had to look. Curiosity *was* his strong point—at least in his mind. He leaned a few inches to the right and examined the stack of recent, three dimensional copies.

At first all he could make out were the tentacles. On their own, they just weren't that bad. Then—he tilted his head to one side—he saw the mouths. Rows of tiny orifices lined the underside of each fleshy limb. A few of these were open. He saw the teeth, and forgot all about sentience. He'd seen enough.

He lunged, and reached one hand for the lid while his other brandished *Galaxy Girl* at the ready. His fingers shook and fumbled with the heavy top. The panic flared again. He squealed and smacked the magazine down, hard, against the machine's bulk. The lid flipped open. Dylan screamed, "AAAAGGGH," and swept the magazine across the copy surface.

A little lump of pink tentacles flew, twisting in mid-air, into the shredder attachment. Dylan slammed his thumb against the control panel. His pulse thumped sharp against his temples. The shredder roared into action and the room exploded with the whir of many blades chewing.

* * *

"What is that?"

Dylan leaned back in the chair and eyed his relief. Shoulder length blue hair framed her pretty face, and her expensive jumpsuit hugged a slim, but curving, figure. She'd never once deigned to make eye contact with the likes of him.

"It's the mail," he answered. "Medical's, not ours." He stood and picked up his brown bag. The sandwich had been delicious, but for some reason, he hadn't managed to nap. He watched her approach the desk and eye the square package sideways. The brown cardboard peeked through here and there between the thick wrappings of cello-tape. The strips criss-crossed the box in every direction. Even after retrieving the pieces from the shredder, even after seeing the mess, he'd wanted to be damned sure. Who knew about things like regeneration these days?

"It's trashed." She sighed as if it had to be his fault and picked up the box.

Dylan flinched slightly as she turned it over. He could hear the bits of tentacle thudding against the sides. He shrugged and walked to the copier, retrieving a small stack of tri-D's.

"What the hell is that?" The girl stared at the images—wads of thick tentacles pressed against glass. Her mouth fell open as he flipped through the copies, slowly, enjoying her reaction to the creature. She'd never said more than three words to him before. He'd seen her cringe when he asked her a question on more than one occasion. Still, she had nice hair. Maybe he should tell her about it. Maybe his bravery would impress her. It just wasn't his style though, was it?

"What is it?" she repeated the question. She leaned forward, close enough that he could smell her perfume.

"My genitals." Dylan's mouth twisted into a smirk. *That* was his style. He watched for her look of shock and horror. He braced himself, tightened his grip on the images of the little bastard, and waited. If he was below her before, he'd damn sure just proven it. Whatever. He needed a good laugh more than a date, anyway.

But when her expression shifted, the look that lingered there could only be described as intrigued. "Really?" she whispered.

He shivered and took a step away from her. He shook his head, clutched his trophies more tightly and turned for the door. He should have taken that transfer. Maybe they had a space for him in the mail room. He carried his copies of the tentacled devil and slid out of Alien-Human relations as fast as his legs could manage. As the door thudded shut between them, he heard the girl call, "See you around, Dylan."

Disgusting. *That* was the problem in an intergalactic society, he thought. You just never knew.

FUELING A JOY RIDE
BY REBECCA BESSER

"You're dad is going to be mad when he finds out you crashed his new cruiser."

"Shut up, Gonk! I won't get in trouble if we don't get caught. Where are we?"

"Earth."

"We can't be! Are you sure?"

Gonk nodded.

We were on a planet that had a surplus of oxygen. The most dangerous substance known to us.

"Do we have suits?"

"I'll check," Gonk said.

He reached behind his seat; his long, black tentacle extended and disappeared. When it returned it held a small, round package.

"Just one," Gonk said.

"There should be two!"

"Calm down, Exas. One is better than none at all."

"But, that means only one of use can leave the cruiser."

"Is the Cloaker working?" Gonk asked.

I reached forward and flipped a switch; a yellow light came on.

"Yes."

"Whoever stays behind will be safe then."

I nodded.

"The one who leaves has to find enough fuel to get us off this planet and home, right?" Gonk asked.

"Yes. Everything seems to be working. We just ran out of fuel."

"That's one good thing about the situation."

"The only one. What does Earth have that we can use for fuel?"

"Um," Gonk said. "I don't know."

"Let's see what Computer can tell us."

I extended a tentacle toward the controls. I compressed the button that activated Computer. The light came on, making the tip of my red tentacle glow brightly as it shone through.

Computer switched on and the monitor appeared above us, glowing bright purple for a moment before a golden female Octus appeared.

"Greetings. How may I be of service to you?"

"We need you to do an environmental scan, looking specifically for possible fuel substances and sources."

"One moment, please, while I process your request. . . Scan in progress."

"You don't think Computer will automatically send out an emergency signal, do you?" Gonk asked.

"I hope not."

"I don't want to have to tell your dad or mine that we took the cruiser on a little joy ride, then crashed on, of all places, Earth!"

I shook my head. "That wouldn't go over well."

"Scan complete. There are three possible fuel sources on the planet Earth. Because of the high level of oxygen detected in the surrounding atmosphere, would you like me to alert Security Command of our location?"

"Do not send an alert. List the fuel sources and where they can be found."

"Three golometics east there is a small settlement called a '*farm*'. There is a creature there, known to the Earth people as a '*chicken*'. Its feathers would make an excellent source of fuel, but you would have to pluck them off of their bodies in order to use them. By my calculations you would need feathers from ten chickens to refuel the ship."

"That sounds time consuming. What's the second option?"

"Fourteen golometics north, there is another '*farm*'. This one has a group of what Earth people call '*turkey*'. You would need the feathers from three '*turkey*' to refuel the ship."

"That's a lot further. What's the third option?"

"Twenty-three golometics south, there is a large cluster of Earth people. They call themselves '*human*'. They congregate at a place called a '*university*' for education purposes. There is a costume one of them wears for ceremonies and gatherings. The person, when dressed in the costume, is usually known as the '*mascot*'. This particular '*mascot*' costume is covered in feathers. The feathers from this suit would also refuel the ship. These three locations are the closest concentrations of fuel available."

"Thank you, Computer."

I reached forward and shut off the computer.

"Which one do you think we should try?"

I thought for a moment. "I think we should try for the closest one first. Then move further away if we need to; it's all about time. We want to get off this planet as quickly as possible."

"I agree," Gonk said. "Do you want me to go and see if I can collect enough feathers? I'm faster than you. . ."

"It's dangerous out there and considering this was all my idea, and it's my fault we're in this mess, I should go."

"I wanted to go! I want to see the planet! It's not likely I'm going to get another opportunity."

"I'll tell you what. . . I'll go first. If there's any trouble, or I can't get the chicken feathers, you can try the next place."

"Okay."

I took the suit from Gonk and put it on.

"I forgot to have Computer give me a scan of a human."

I reached forward and turned Computer back on, and waited patiently for her to boot.

"Greetings. How may I be of service to you?"

"Computer, please load a scan of a human onto this suit card. Also, add the locations of the fuel sources and any other information we might need."

I inserted the small square card and waited.

"Upload complete."

"Thanks Computer," I said, switching her off again.

I took out the card and inserted it into the card holder located in the front center of the suit, then pushed the small diamond button to activate it.

"Wow," Gonk said.

"What?"

"You look strange. Is that what a human looks like?"

"I don't know. I've never seen a human."

"You look pale, have only two arms, and two other limbs to stand on," Gonk said, and grinned. "You have some kind of fuzzy stuff on your head that looks like the fungus that grew on my grandmothers left overs last week, and you have two small, beady eyes."

"That does sound weird. At least I'll have an idea what humans look like, if I should see one."

"Hopefully you don't meet one."

I stepped over beside the door and looked at myself in the reflector; a young human male stared back at me.

He had light yellow fuzz on the top of his head, dark blue eyes, and light peach skin. He was dressed in a black shirt and blue pants that were made of a heavy material; on his feet he wore a pair of black leather boots.

"I look young."

"Maybe you reflect a human at your current age," Gonk said. "Sixteen or seventeen sun revolutions."

"That could be. I'd better go. The sooner we collect the fuel, the sooner we can return home."

"Be careful. I'll turn on the Cloaker as soon as you're outside."

I nodded, opened the door, and stepped into the air lock chamber. I waited until the door behind me closed completely and the green light came on before I opened the door that would leave me exposed to Earth's atmosphere. I held my breath as it slide open, hoping the suit would do its job and I wouldn't burst into flames.

Nothing happened.

I sighed with relief and stepped out of the cruiser.

I turned back to look at the cruiser and it wasn't there; the Cloaker was doing its job.

I faced east and took off at a run. Three golometics was a decent distance, but with seven legs it didn't take long. I was glad the suit only projected the image of a human and didn't actually change me into human form, as I would have lost most of my legs and the speed I could accomplish with them.

It wasn't long before I approached the 'farm'. I saw the 'chickens' Computer had told me about. I warily looked around to see if there were any humans close by.

The coast was clear.

I walked up to one of the 'chickens' and bent forward to pick it up. It screeched, flapped its wings violently, and darted away. I advanced on another with the same results.

I approached yet another chicken and grabbed it. It flapped its wings for a moment and tried to get away, but I held on.

I wrapped two tentacles around the its small, flailing body and yanked out its feathers furiously; they flew into the air around me in a white cloud of fluff.

After I'd finished with one, I grabbed another and gave it the same treatment. I was about to snatch a third when I heard a loud voice coming toward me. Someone was shouting.

"You crazy kid! What are you doing to my chickens?"

I heard a loud boom.

I turned to look at what was making the noise and saw a human male, much older than the male I presented. He was pointing a booming staff at me and he looked angry.

"Put the chicken down, boy," he growled.

I released the chicken. I stared at him for a moment and decided my best bet would be to run away.

I took a deep breath, turned sharply, and wheeled back the way I'd come. I heard another loud boom. The man yelled again, but I was too far away to hear what he said.

I'd forgotten to bring any of the feathers. Of course it wasn't like I'd had time to gather them before I left. The human had been extremely threatening.

He must have wanted to keep the chicken feathers for his own cruiser, I thought.

I returned to the ship.

Gonk was standing by the door as I came in.

"Did you bring any feathers?"

I told him what had happened.

"Wow! Sounds like humans really are dangerous. I'm not sure I want to go out there now, but I did say I wanted to take a turn. Let me have the suit."

I took off the suit and Gonk put it on.

"How do I look?"

"You look the same as I did. Be careful. Here take this bag to bring the feathers back in."

Gonk nodded, took the bag I'd pulled out of a small side compartment, and went out into the air lock. I watched him as the door slid closed.

After he stepped out onto Earth, I flipped the switch to activate the Cloaker once again. I saw him glance back and then take off to the north.

He was gone for quite some time. While I was waiting I tuned our Receptor to see if I could find a signal of any kind. I had luck, but wasn't happy with what I heard, considering the only signals I could pick up were from Earth.

There was what sounded like a news bulletin about a young male terrorizing chickens. The description of the young man matched that of the image the suit projected. I hoped this news would not reach the area Gonk was in.

I waited anxiously for him to return. A half hour later I saw Gonk running toward me. I turned off the Cloaker and hit the button to open the outer door.

"Did you get anything?"

Gonk sighed. "I have feathers from one '*turkey*'. I tried to get more but a human saw me, called me 'Feather Wrangler,' and then tried to trap me. They said something about turning me over to the local authorities for something done to chickens."

"I heard about it through the Receptor. There was a news bulletin with the description of our projected human."

"Humans are crazy. A female human tried to stab me with a long, sharp, forked tool, and a male human tried to tie me up. But, I let their turkeys out of their holding cell and the humans went chasing after them and seemed to forget about me."

"At least you got away! Plus, you brought back some feathers! That's better than I did. Let's give them to Computer and see how much more we'll need."

Together we took the feathers and loaded them into the fuel conversion tank; Computer automatically converted the feathers into useful fuel.

When Computer came on and said we only had a quarter of a tank of fuel, I sighed and closed my eye. We would have to go to the third source. The hardest one. It was far away and there would be many humans to contend with. It was also my turn to go.

"Give me the suit."

"What if they recognize you as the 'Feather Wrangler'?"

"It's a risk I'll take. We either get fuel or we're stuck here."

"We could always send for help," Gonk said. "We would get in trouble, but at least we wouldn't die."

"You're right. But I would rather just get home with no one knowing we'd ever been here."

I turned and headed for the air lock. Action was the only way to get home. Action was the only course that would save our lives.

I headed south. It seemed like no time and I was there. Humans were everywhere: male, female, old, and young. At first I hung back, unsure how I should proceed. After the incident with the older man earlier, I wasn't sure if these humans were going to be hostile or not.

I walked in amongst them. A couple glanced at me and then went back to what they were doing.

I approached the building where the intelligence Computer had given me said the suit was housed. I glanced around nervously. If the old man was so possessive of his fuel source, would these humans be too? Considering the number of them around, they had to need a large supply of fuel.

I paused as I reached for the handle of the door.

What if the suit was for a religious ceremony? I thought. *Hadn't Computer said it was used for ceremonies? Maybe they wear it and do a dance for their gods. . . Would their fuel god be angered if I took the suit, or even just the feathers from it?*

"Hey, man," a male said behind me. "Are you going in or what?"

I stepped aside, flustered and confused.

He went through the door shaking his head.

I stood there for a moment thinking. *Should I risk the possible bad luck of stealing feathers from a ceremonial garment?*

I decided it would be worth the risk and quickly went through the door before I could change my mind. I hurried through the passageways to the room that housed the feather suit.

The door was locked.

I stood there, staring at the door, wondering how I was going to get it open without drawing attention.

"You must be Mike's replacement," a woman said behind me. "I was hoping you'd get here before the game."

Game? Replacement? I nodded; I didn't know what else to do.

"Let's get you suited up. Is this your first time being a mascot?"

"Yes."

Mascot? Could I have really just gotten that lucky? Were they just going to give me the suit I was after?

"The costume is in the closet over there. I'll leave you to get dressed."

I watched her leave with a mixture of excitement and dread.

I rushed over to the closet, threw open the door, and ripped the suit from its hanger. I grabbed the large head covering from the shelf above and returned to the door. I ran out, down the hall, and breezed through the door I'd entered as someone opened it.

I heard a shout behind me, but didn't slow down.

I was almost clear of the humans and their educational gathering when someone pointed at me and shouted.

"It's the Feather Wrangler!"

Someone else yelled, "Get him!"

Soon a hoard of humans was chasing me. I dropped the head cover. It flew up into the air and landed backwards on one of the male humans' heads, blinding him. He fell, tripping the others.

I made my way back to the ship, sighing with relief as it came into view.

I entered the portal, breathing hard.

"You were gone so long," Gonk said, "I thought they'd caught you."

I shook my head and handed Gonk the feather garment.

"Here, see if it's enough fuel," I said and sat down, peeling off the suit.

He put it in the conversion tank; Computer turned on and sighed.

"You have refueled the ship. Would you like to prepare for take off?"

"Yes. Take off and head for home."

"What happened?"

I told him while we strapped in and prepared to depart.

"Maybe we should've changed the projection of the human before you left," Gonk said.

"I wish we would've thought of that before."

"Doesn't matter now. We're going home."

As I pushed buttons and turned knobs to prepare for take off, I accidentally bump the Receptor, turning it on. It blasted out a new news bulletin as we took to the air.

"The Feather Wrangler has struck again, stealing the mascot costume from a local university. It was an antique and has been passed down for many generations. It was going to be used in a special welcoming ceremony tonight. . ."

We flew out of range and didn't hear the rest.

"I hope we make it home before that ceremony."

"Why?" Gonk asked.

"Because I think the costume was for a ceremony to worship their god. If we don't make it home before he knows it's gone, he might get angry and hurt us."

Gonk stared at me. "Why did you take it then? We've had enough bad luck. What if this god knows it was us and curses our planet? What are we supposed to do then? Our dads are going to be so mad!"

"We don't have to tell them. Let's just wait and see what happens. We still might make it home before the god catches us."

We made it home without incident. My dad didn't even notice the cruiser had been gone for a couple of hours.

* * *

Six months later, something happened that scared me so much I almost told my dad what had happened.

A trade ship returned from a voyage that took them somewhat close to Earth. Close enough they were able to pick up a transmission. I didn't hear all of it, but it was something about a missing costume and the school it had belonged to getting flooded when a huge storm came though. The traders had joked about the gods being angry with them for losing their ceremonial attire.

They went on to say there was also a fuel shortage throughout the empire.

Was this all because I had made the fuel god angry when I stole the suit?

I never did tell my dad. I didn't even tell Gonk. But, to this day, I wonder if it was all my fault. Could a joy ride really cause that much trouble in the universe?

HEART OF A SOLDIER
BY REBECCA BESSER

Docking the shuttle took all of Zyle's concentration. This was only his second training flight and he didn't want to mess up and have to start the course over again.

"Good job, Zyle," Instructor Handor said. "That was a good flight. I'm surprised how well you're able to do the maneuvers. Most students don't master those until they've taken the course at least twice."

"Couldn't be the extra training my dad makes me take in the simulation capsule, could it?" Zyle asked, laughing. "Not everyone has the military obsessed father I do."

Instructor Handor snorted. "Yeah, but your 'military obsessed father' has done wonders for the Jupiter Mining Base. The JMB was in shambles when he arrived."

Zyle sighed. "I know, he reminds me of it often."

Handor laughed. "Well, it was no small accomplishment. He brought scientists and cutting edge technology to what was once just a mining operation. JMB is flourishing with him in charge."

Zyle shut down the shuttle and removed his training badge, as well as his Datafile-Attachable-Memory stick, from the consol of the training shuttle.

Stepping out, Zyle surveyed the dock. There was a large shuttle unloading a new group of students who had come to JMB for the promise of a free education; scholarships in exchange for an internship on one of the research bases, or a spot in the military.

"Yes, indeed," Zyle said over his shoulder to Handor. "He has brought a lot to JMB. He's hoping I'll do the same when he passes the reins."

"Resigned yourself to it, then, have you?" Handor asked, typing the last of his training notes into the small fiberoptic board he carried.

"I guess," Zyle said with a shrug. "I don't really have a choice. He won't let me go back to Earth to take the courses I want. He's bound and determined I'll be a military man like him."

Handor slapped Zyle on the back as he walked by. "There are worse things you could be."

Zyle shook his head and retrieved his bag from the shuttle, dropping his DAM-stick and badge into it. Flinging the pack over his shoulder, he headed toward the dock exit, colliding with one of the new students.

"Oh, excuse me," Zyle said, reaching out to steady the young woman he'd almost knocked down. "I didn't see you."

"Sorry, I wasn't paying attention," she said at the same time.

They both laughed.

"Are you all right?" Zyle asked.

"Yes, yes, I'm fine."

Zyle couldn't help by stare at the young woman. She was short, around five feet tall, with brown hair, and huge, dark brown eyes.

"Um. . . " the woman said uncomfortably, tucking her long hair behind her ear. "I better get going, before the group leaves and I get lost."

"Huh?" Zyle asked. "Oh, okay. Sorry again."

She giggled and hurried to catch up with the group of new students who would be taken on a tour of the JMB, where they would learn about the base and its operation.

Zyle stepped forward when the door closed behind her and he realized he hadn't even asked her what her name was.

Slapping himself on the forehead, he made his way out through the exit and looked after the group, hoping to speak with her again. She was at the front of the crowd, right by the guide.

He sighed and turned to go to his dorm room.

Zyle couldn't think of anything except the woman's beautiful eyes and sweet smile. Somehow he made it to his room. Pressing his palm to the announcing pad that doubled as an identity scanner, he stepped inside.

"How did the flight go today?" Hex teased. "Hit any rocks? Or did you just blast them out of your way?"

"Ha, ha, ha," Zyle said to his roommate. "There were no rocks, but if there had been, I would have handled them."

"You think the simulation capsule is anything like the real thing?" Hex asked.

"I don't know," Zyle said, stowing his stuff on the shelves above his bunk. "I hope I never have to find out. Handor says that not even the most experienced pilots are ready for rock storms; most don't come back."

"See why I took intelligence instead of all that combat stuff?" Hex asked. "This way, I'm safe and sound away from the action."

Zyle laughed. "Except if you get assigned to a shuttle. Then you'll have to be in the thick of it and not have any control. I'd rather have some control over the situation, if I have to be in it."

Hex grunted. "There's an important message for you."

Zyle raised his eyebrow at Hex, who seemed to be engrossed in his homework. "Did you read it?"

Hex shrugged, but didn't look up.

Zyle sat down in front of the fiberoptic panel in the corner of his side of the room and proceed to check his messages. Most were personal messages from friends, a couple of reminders from classes, but that wasn't what Hex was referring to. There was one from the correspondence school Zyle had applied to.

He read it, then read it again. They denied his enrollment, saying that the in-class assignments were impossible because there wasn't a literature course available where he was currently going to school. His dream of studying the language, culture, and history he'd come from was officially impossible.

Zyle turned off the panel, got up, and lay down on his bunk with his arms behind his head; he stared up at nothing.

"Sorry, man," Hex said quietly. "I know you were hoping to at least take a correspondence course."

"Yeah," Zyle said.

"Maybe they'll have a teacher here in a couple of years for literature and then you can take it."

Zyle didn't respond. He stood and walked out of the room without a backwards glance. Turning to the right, he walked through the corridors blindly, not caring where he was going. Nothing was working out the way he wanted, but everything seemed to be conspiring against him to his father's will.

Without even realizing it, Zyle wandered down to the next level and into the Fountain Room; it was where he always went to think. The soothing sounds of water helped him to relax and cleared his mind when things were bothering him. Today, he needed that peace.

He sat in the corner, where he had a good view of the fountain and of Jupiter. Staring out at the planet, he watched the lightning flash in the depth of its Great Red Eye. It had always fascinated him, the storms that ravaged the planet, and how it seemed to remain the same despite the constant changes. Zyle sometimes wished he could harness that peace within the storm and have better control of the things that influenced his life.

* * *

The next day Zyle sat in his first class, staring out into space, waiting for another boring session of information he already knew.

He heard a long, low whistle behind him.

"Look at her," Hex said, as he leaned forward and punched Zyle in the arm.

Zyle sighed and turned his attention to the front of the class, where a young woman in a yellow dress was talking to Mr. Lynvix. It took him a moment to register that the young woman was the same one from the dock.

"Wonder what she's doing in Mining and Operation?" Zyle mumbled to himself, frowning.

"I don't know and I don't care," Hex said. "At least she's an improvement on the view."

Zyle shook his head, watching the exchange between the woman and the teacher. It wasn't going good, if the expression on Mr. Lynvix's face was anything to go by. Eventually he motioned for her to be seated, and everything seemed to be settled.

Mr. Lynvix turned to the class and began speaking.

Hurriedly, Zyle removed the translator ear piece from the tip of his DAM-stick and inserted it in his left ear. The translator was a new technology and he still forgot to use it from time to time. Mr. Lynvix was Swedish and he always taught in his native language, although he spoke fluent English.

"I trust you've all inserted your DAM-sticks into your panels, and have pulled up the JMB map," Mr. Lynvix was saying. "We'll begin at. . ."

The young woman raised her hand.

"Yes?" Mr. Lynvix asked impatiently.

"I can't understand what you're saying."

"No one explained the translator or the DAM-stick to you?" he replied in English, disbelief and frustration apparent in every word.

"You should know how the DAM-stick works before you come to class. If you would like to take the course for the operation of the DAM-stick, please go and do so now. I don't have time to teach you the basics of the panel, the sticks, and their function. This is an advanced course and you're wasting my time."

Zyle could see that Mr. Lynvix was upsetting the woman. During his rant she stared down at the DAM-stick, which lay in her palm. When she turned to retrieve her bag, he saw that her cheeks were wet with tears.

"Mr. Lynvix," Zyle said, standing. He locked his right hand around his left wrist behind his back, stuck out his chest, planted his feet shoulder width apart, and looked straight ahead.

Zyle could feel Mr. Lynvix's eyes traveling over him, starting at his pulled back wheat blonde hair, proceeding over his sleeveless black cadet's shirt, down over his baggy black pants, and shining black boots.

"Yes, Mr. Nexthis," Mr. Lynvix barked. "What can I help you with?"

Zyle saw the girl freeze half way out of her seat, then sit back down.

"Sir, I wouldn't mind sharing a panel with the young woman for this class. I would also request she be assigned a tutor to help her get up to speed, since she wishes to take this course."

"Well, Mr. Nexthis," Mr. Lynvix ground out. "Since you seem to have taken so much interest in her welfare, you'll tutor her. But know this, I expect her to be up to 'speed' by the end of the week. That gives you two days to teach her what she needs to know or I'll send her to basic lessons!"

"Thank you, sir."

Grabbing his stuff, Zyle unplugged his DAM-stick and marched to where the young woman sat. She stared up at him with frightened eyes, tears still clinging to her dark lashes.

"Hello again, I'm Zyle," he said gently. "If you'll come with me, we'll move to a conference table that we can share. What's your name?"

"Aphrila," she murmured as she rose and picked up her belongings, before following him to the front right corner of the room.

Zyle could feel Mr. Lynvix's eyes on them. He pulled out a chair for Aphrila and waited for her to be seated. He sat beside her and inserted his DAM-stick into the panel, setting it up as fast as his fingers would fly. He inserted her DAM-stick into the slot next to his and quietly helped her set up her password, learn about her translator, and even helped her insert her ear piece.

After Zyle got everything set up, Mr. Lynvix seemed to ignore them for the rest of the class. Droning on and on about the amazing structure they lived in, which allowed them to collect the hydrogen and helium from Jupiter's atmosphere.

It was a good thing he wasn't covering anything new that day, because Zyle wouldn't have been able to concentrate. Aphrila smelled way too good, and she had a quick, soft smile that was always genuine.

Zyle had a fleeting thought that if he wasn't careful he could fall in love with her.

Class was over before they knew it.

Aphrila smiled one of her smiles and thanked Zyle for helping her. They set up a time to meet later in the Fountain Room, before they left for their next classes.

Hex accosted Zyle in the hall.

"Man," he said, wrapping his arm around Zyle's neck. "You really had balls today, standing up to Mr. Lynx! I thought for sure he was going to blow a gasket. His face turned four shades of red. Hopefully this doesn't make it back to your dad. – he'll be pissed."

Zyle stopped and turned to Hex, knocking his arm away.

"Why," he hissed through clenched teeth, "would my dad be angry about me standing up for someone who was weaker than I am? Isn't that the whole point of being a solider, to protect those who are weaker? To stand up for what's right and just?!"

Zyle inched closer and closer to Hex's face with each word. When he finished they were nose to nose, even though he was a good four inches shorter than Zyle's six-foot height.

"Easy," Hex said. "Easy, Man. I didn't mean to set you off."

He looked around at the students who had stopped to stare. They were probably hoping for a fight.

Zyle swung his gaze toward the crowd; they quickly dispersed.

Hex cleared his throat and grabbed Zyle's arm.

"Let's get to our next class," Hex said, pulling Zyle along. "We don't want to be late."

Shrugging off Hex's grip, Zyle walked beside him into their next classroom.

* * *

Later that evening Zyle sat in the Fountain Room watching droplets of water rise up into the air and fall back into the pool.

"I hope I didn't keep you waiting," Aphrila's now familiar voice said from beside him.

"No, I haven't been here long. Did you bring your DAM-sticks?"

"Yes," she said, reaching into her bag. "I have them right here. I programed all of them with passwords. Thank you for taking the time to help me. I should've taken the basic courses first, I guess."

She looked down at the toe of her shoe, seeming to find it intensely interesting. Then she looked back at Zyle and smiled brightly.

"Are we going to study here?" she asked, motioning to the fountain. "Or do we need to go somewhere else?"

"We can study here," Zyle said. "Pull up a chair. First, I think we should get to know each other."

"I agree," Aphrila said. "Have you lived here long?"

"Twelve years," he sighed and she laughed. "My dad runs J5 sector. It's the sector that controls the stability of the base and how it's run. We call it J5-base, because it's the base within the base. What brings you all the way to Jupiter?"

"Well," Aphrila said, biting her lip and tucking her hair behind her ear, "I was a medical student on Earth. I heard there was some cutting edge medical research here on the JMB, so I transferred. The military always has the newest and the best."

"So, you want to poke and prod us," he teased. "Well, I hope you learn what you want to know."

"Me too, but first I have to figure out how these DAM-sticks work."

Zyle proceeded to explain the Datafile-Attachable-Memory sticks to her in greater detail. He also explained how the base worked, and its functions. He knew that she'd gotten some of this information the day before on her tour, but he took the time to answer her questions.

"Zyle, yesterday they said most of the protein in the food here is made from peanuts. What do people with food allergies eat?"

Zyle grinned. "They've developed a vaccine that people with allergies are given before they arrive. They don't have any problems after that."

"You mean, they've actually discovered a vaccine for food allergies?" Aphrila asked, surprised. "Have they discovered any other cures?"

"Hmm, I think I've heard something about a stone with healing properties."

"What does it cure?" she asked excitedly. "How does it work? Where did they find it? What are the statistics? Where is it?"

Zyle laughed at her enthusiasm. "I think the lab is on one of the moons. On the Ganymede moon, I believe. It's slightly magnetic. They found a large expanse of salt water trapped under the surface, surrounded by ice. When they were mining to the core they found a thin layer of some kind of rock. That's all I know. I'm not much into medicine."

"That's amazing! Is there any way to see a piece of the rock?" Aphrila asked, excitedly. "Can I go to the lab, on the moon? What did you say the name of it was?"

"Ganymede."

"Is there any way to get there?"

"You could rent a shuttle-car, but it would cost a lot, and you would have to get clearance to visit the lab. Not to mention that you would have to wait until the moon is in the right position in orbit."

She was about to ask something else when Hex sauntered up to the table.

"Hey," he said. "How's the studying going? Are you learning lots of new stuff about the JMB?"

"Yes. I've learned a lot, and now I have to go," Aphrila said as she swept all of her DAM-sticks into her bag and stood. "Zyle, thank you for taking the time to help me."

She smiled briefly at Hex and darted for the exit.

"What do you want?" Zyle asked Hex absently.

"Oh, I just wondered how it was going." Hex grinned as he came around the table and took the seat Aphrila had vacated. "I found some information on your friend."

"Oh? Snooping through personal files again, were we?"

"No, just message transfers and interactive conversations. Personal files are way too easy to access. I figure since I'm taking intelligence and computer programing I might as well use my skills."

Zyle looked at Hex and shook his head.

"She's a medical student. She just arrived from Earth yesterday."

"She told me," Zyle said mildly.

"But, what she probably didn't tell you is that she's dying of cancer, and her parents let her come here because she wanted to see the Universe before she died. She's only seventeen, you know. . ."

Hex rambled on, spilling his information like a little kid pouring himself a drink for the first time. It all made sense now. She was here to see if she could get her hands on a piece of that stone.

Zyle couldn't breathe. He'd just realized that he'd indeed fallen in love with this young woman, only to find out she was dying.

Standing abruptly, blind to the shocked expression on Hex's face, he knew what he had to do. He went to see his dad.

* * *

Two hours later Zyle was pacing in his room, mad at his father.

He couldn't wait a whole week to go over to the lab with Mom. What if Aphrila didn't have that long?

Grabbing his pack, he hefted it over his shoulder and left his room. He headed to the female section of the dormitory.

Zyle pushed the announcing pad twice with his palm and waited for Aphrila to answer. She frowned in confusion as the panel slid back and she saw him standing in the hall.

"I'll take you to Ganymede. Hurry and get everything you'll need for a two-day trip."

She stared at him, blinking like an owl.

"You know," she whispered. "How do you know? I didn't tell anyone."

"Doesn't matter. Just get your stuff."

"But, how are we going to get a shuttle-car?"

Zyle held up his training badge, grinning. "I have some hours left."

Her eyes lit up and she packed quickly.

They made their way down to the shuttle dock and used his training card to secure a transport.

Before long they were clear of the JMB and sailing through space toward where Ganymede would be in a couple of hours.

"The hardest part is going to be convincing the scientists to let us land."

"Why are you doing this for me?" Aphrila asked, turning to face Zyle.

He shifted to look her in the eye. The tears he saw there almost undid him. Should he tell her the truth? Or make something up? His brain panicked and came up blank.

He decided on the truth.

"I've fallen in love with you. I know I haven't known you long, but I love you. When I heard you had cancer and might die, I thought I would too."

Aphrila opened her mouth to speak.

Zyle pressed his finger against her lips. "Let me finish, please. I don't know if we can get you a piece of that stone, but we're definitely going to try."

She smiled and he could feel her lips move under his finger. Gently, she gripped his wrist, moving his hand.

"Zyle, I'm not sick – my mother is. She's dying of cancer. They've tried multiple treatments on her. None of them helped. That's why I'm here, to get a stone, to see if it'll do for her what the other treatments won't."

Zyle was shocked. He looked up at the ceiling of the piloting cabin and took deep breaths. He'd risked his relationship with his dad, his education, and his future on getting something for someone he'd never even met. He was shaping up to be a pretty good soldier after all.

"Are you mad?"

"No, just confused."

Gently Aphrila turned his face to look at her, cupping his cheek in her hand. She leaned forward and kissed him.

"I think I'm in love with you too," she whispered as she leaned back slightly.

Zyle pulled her toward him and kissed her again.

"Let's go get that stone," he said, pulling away and grinning.

They were almost to the moon. It floated in front of them, its gray surface scarred and pitted, growing larger and larger with each passing minute.

"Is that Ganymede?" Aphrila asked.

"Yes," Zyle said. "I'm going to have to dump some fuel. I have to convince them to let us land, they'll only let us if we have an emergency."

She nodded.

Flicking a couple switches, Zyle dumped fuel from the tanks and flipped the switch that would send their distress signal to the medical lab.

Almost instantly they responded.

"This is Ganymede Medical Lab 332. What's your emergency?"

"I've lost fuel. We don't have enough to go to another moon. I only have enough left for five minutes."

There was a long pause.

"Proceed to dock 15B. You'll get more instructions after landing."

"They're letting us dock," Zyle said. "But, don't expect a warm welcome."

* * *

They were met at dock 15B by four armed men in military uniforms.

"Come with us," one of the men said. Zyle recognized him as a sergeant by the bright blue strip that ran vertically down the middle of his sleeveless black shirt.

Nodding, Zyle gently pressed his hand to the small of Aphrila's back. She glanced up at him with anxious eyes. He smiled down at her briefly and returned his gaze to the men.

"As you wish," Zyle said.

As they walked forward the front two men turned to walk in front of them, while the other two spun on their heel to follow closely behind.

They wove through multiple passageways that seemed to be taking them under ground. Finally they came to a door at the dead end of a hall. The sergeant punched in a code and the door panels slide open. He motioned for them to go in.

They stepped inside a spacious office with a lounge area and a large desk.

"Please take a seat, the Captain will be with your shortly," the sergeant said.

The door closed behind them and they were left alone.

"What do you think they're going to do with us?" Aphrila asked.

"I don't know," Zyle said, frowning.

They sat together on the couch in the lounge area and waited.

Aphrila shifted nervously and looked around.

"It'll be okay," Zyle reassured her.

She looked up at him and he winked, reaching for her hand. Holding it firmly, Zyle rubbing his thumb back and forth over her knuckles.

They both jumped when the door opened and a short, gray-haired man entered..

He just stood there, looking at them like they were an exhibit. His black shirt had a bright red strip going across it horizontally. He was the captain they were waiting for.

"We've been expecting you," he said, finally. "Commander-in-Chief Nexthis sent word of your plans."

Zyle snorted. "Figures."

The captain took his time looking over Aphrila, making her shift in her seat uncomfortably. Zyle squeezed her hand, reminding her she wasn't alone.

"You don't look like you have cancer, my dear," the man said in a surprisingly gentle voice.

"I don't. My mother does."

The captain sat down in a chair across from them, rubbing his chin.

"The stones we found may or may not help someone with cancer," he stated. "They draw toxins out of the body. We've been studying their effects for awhile, but haven't tested them on anyone with cancer. I'd be open to doing a lab study on your mother, if she's willing. She would have to live here at the lab, so we can monitor her. How long would it take her to get here?"

Aphrila stared at the gray-haired man, her mouth hanging open.

"Really?" she asked in disbelief. "I suppose she could be here in a week."

"Great," the man said, standing. "Excuse me, I haven't introduced myself. I'm Captain Bratyn, a medical scientist. The military has given me opportunities to conduct some cutting edge experiments, which have saved many lives. That reminds me, Aphrila, Commander-in-Chief Nexthis sent me your file. When I heard you were coming, I requested it. There will be an internship opening up next year and I wondered if you would like to apply for it. You certainly have high enough grades to qualify."

"I would be honored," Aphrila said solemnly.

Zyle tried not to grin as he watched her try to take in all the new information and opportunities. It was obvious she was overwhelmed.

"Sounds good," Captain Bratyn said, going to his desk and typing something into his fiberoptic panel. "I've sent a message to all your instructors at the JMB. They'll need to give comments on your performance. When that's done, you'll be considered."

"Thank you, Captain," Aphrila said.

"I have something else for you," Captain Bratyn said, pulling two strings with small pieces of shining stone out of his pants-pocket. "Wear them every day and have a physical each month. These are small pieces of the healing stone we've found."

"Thank you," Aphrila and Zyle said at the same time, taking their gifts.

Zyle looked down at the small piece of stone nestled against his palm. It was the sized of his thumb nail – flat and round – a quarter of an inch thick. From the side it was clear, from the front it looked like creamy, reflective glass. Where it contacted his skin it turned black.

"Why's it turning black?" Zyle asked.

"That's the stone drawing toxins from your skin. Wash the stone with soap and water whenever needed. The cleaner it is the better it'll work. We've been wearing them for six months, with no ill effects," Captain Bratyn said with a wink. "Sorry, but I have to run, wasn't expecting company, you know. Have a safe trip back."

The Captain smiled and left.

Another man, one of the men from the escort, came in immediately and announced that their shuttle-car was ready to return to JMB. He alone escorted them to dock 15B.

"We've refueled your shuttle, is there anything else you need for your return trip to the JMB?" he asked politely.

"No, I think we have everything we'll need."

Zyle held Aphrila's elbow as she stepped up into the shuttle-car.

"There's a cluster of rock fragments in the atmosphere between here and the JMB," he said. "We dumped some rock on the other side of the moon yesterday. The fragments are just starting to come around and head toward Jupiter. We wouldn't have done it if we'd known you were coming. Next time you should wait for clearance before you head out. There are many reasons to plan a trip, some of them are for your own safety."

"I'll remember that," Zyle said.

He nodded, turned, and left, closing the portal behind him.

Zyle frowned. The rock cluster couldn't be too bad, or they would have asked them to stay. Wouldn't they?

They were quickly on our way, sailing free of the Ganymede lab heading toward the JMB.

"That wasn't as bad as I thought it would be," Aphrila breathed.

"No, wasn't bad at all," Zyle said, his mind on the possibility of trouble.

He saw her out of the corner of his eye, rubbing the stone that now hung around her neck.

"I hope these work. It would be wonderful to have found something to cure cancer. It's such a terrible disease. Many centuries of research and development and it still kills."

Zyle nodded and was about to reply when a warning alarm began to sound. Cursing under his breath, he silenced the alarms and checked the control panel.

"What's wrong? What's happening?" Aphrila asked.

"I think we'll be in for a bumpy ride. It seems we're getting close to the rocks the soldier warned me about. You might want to strap in."

Zyle tried to keep my tone light so he wouldn't worry her. The situation was much more dangerous than he was letting on. The rocks were heading directly at them, and because of the magnetic gravity of Jupiter, they were going to be pulled right into the thick of them.

Strapping himself in, and glancing to the side to make sure she did too, he put on a helmet with a fiberoptic visor that would allow him to see everything floating around outside.

Zyle cursed again as he noticed how many rocks there were, and at the massive size of them. He would have to try to steer around most of them, knowing the guns wouldn't be able to break those big boys up with one blast.

Flicking a switch, Zyle started to charge up the guns. Praying they would be ready before they got too close.

He shifted his gaze between the front window and the light on the panel, which would illuminate when the guns energized.

The rocks were upon them and the light hadn't come on.

"Close your eyes and hold on tight," Zyle said.

He yanked the control stick to the left and they swung violently sideways, missing the first big rock by a hair. Shoving the control stick down he tried to fly underneath the next one. The rocks were too close together. The front of the shuttle-car cleared the rubble, but it hit the back. A loud scrapping noise and then an even louder boom emanated from behind them.

Aphrila screamed.

Quickly, Zyle turned off the emergency alarm when it sounded. He needed to break the cabin away from the rest of the shuttle-car. It had been designed as an escape pod, but it wouldn't save them in this storm. It would likely kill them when they ejected from the main body.

Scanning the rocks, Zyle saw a small opening, to the right, above them. If he could get them over there, and point them up, they'd have a chance.

Finally the light on the panel lit up, announcing the readiness of the weapons.

Slamming all of his weight against the control stick, Zyle steered them to the right. They changed direction sluggishly and got bumped by another rock, throwing them into a spiraling spin.

Without even thinking, Zyle fired the high-blast energy guns and ejected the pilot pod at the same time. He hoped the blast would move anything that might be in the way and propel them safely beyond the rock cluster.

Aphrila screamed again; she sounded close to hysteria.

Looking around, Zyle was grateful to see his reflexes had done them some good; they were now flying above the cluster. He could see the remains of their shuttle-car being ricocheted violently from rock to rock. The fuel cell was breached and the whole thing exploded, pushing them even further away.

Sighing, knowing they'd blessedly made it out of the worst of the danger, Zyle allowed himself a glance at Aphrila. She was weeping, sobbing uncontrollably, and shaking like a leaf.

Reaching over, he pried her hand from her arm rest; her grip was so tight she'd left imprints in the thick, hard padding.

"It's okay," Zyle said softly. "We're out of the rocks. We'll be all right."

She kept weeping and gasping.

"Aphrila," he said sternly. "Look at me!"

Slowly, her head turned in his direction.

"We're going to be all right. I'm going to set the auto-pilot and it'll take us to the JMB. We'll be there in twenty minutes or so. Everything is going to be okay."

"I . . . I . . . Okay," she stammered.

Zyle reached over and set the auto-pilot.

He undid his straps and leaned over, undoing Aphrila's. Gently, he lifted her out of her seat and into his lap. Wrapping his arms around her, he held her tight until she stopped shaking.

"Are you all right now?"

Aphrila nodded against his chest.

They traveled the rest of the way to the JMB in silence.

Thoughts of the risk they'd taken kept churning through Zyle's mind.

Was it worth risking their lives? Could these small pieces of stone do all they hoped? Would it cure cancer? Would it keep them healthy?

* * *

Six months later, Zyle stood in the shuttle bay and watched Aphrila welcome her mother back to the JMB. He couldn't believe the transformation. The healing stone had taken away any and all traces of her illness.

"So, son," Zyle's dad said, coming up behind him and putting his hand on his shoulder. "What do you think she's going to say when you tell her you two are engaged?"

Zyle laughed. "I think she'll be pleased. At least that's what Aphrila keeps telling me."

"Has Aphrila heard from the Ganymede Medical Lab?"

Zyle sighed. "She hasn't heard anything yet. If she does get accepted for the internship we'll have to decide where to live. I hate to think we would have to live apart for a year or more. But, I know I'll do what I have to do."

Dad laughed, and slapped Zyle on the back. "You won't have to. I'm transferring you over there."

Zyle frowned. "What? We don't even know if she's been accepted yet!"

Dad winked. "She has, and so have you. Consider it a wedding present."

"Thanks, Dad," Zyle said in shocked surprise.

"You're welcome," Dad said. "I'm proud of you. I know you never wanted to be a military man, but you've got quite a heart for it, soldier."

"What're you two conspiring about?" Aphrila asked, as she and her mother walked over.

"We'll tell all at dinner," Zyle teased and kissed the tip of her nose.

As they all walked down the hall, Zyle thought about the risks he'd taken to help others and how he'd benefited from those risks, as well. Smiling, Zyle realized his dad was right. He did have the heart of a solider.

THE GIFT OF INNOCENCE, THE TRAGEDY OF IGNORANCE...
BY JAMES CONWAY

Boon looked down at his fellow Maerrisian, who was now strapping him into the small interior of the drop pod. Unlike he, Krogna was born of low-line blood, thus happened to be small, skinny, and weak. Despite this, Krogna had brains, discipline, and a good heart. Today Boon thought Krogna was oddly cold. It was a big day for the Outer Alliance. A decision had to be made after all these years of sluggish debate. Tensions ran high.

He noticed Krogna looking up at him with those small, dark, deep-set eyes. It was often hard knowing what went on when someone happened to be a third of your height. Krogna looked concerned.

"Munalie ecca unno," said the small grey creature peering up with crooked neck. There was ice in his voice. Nobody took today anything but serious, time for games now over.

"Munalie ecca unno," he repeated, this time kicking Boon on the shin.

"Ourg, ourg," Boon pleaded, before pressing a small green button on a collar around his neck, which lit up a few shades brighter than his own natural skin tone.

The grey waited before he clicked his fingers frantically. "Doo-doo, faryoup."

"Maips taka," whispered Boon.

The grey slapped his forehead loud enough for others in the near corridor to hear. "Faryoup, faryoup, FAROUP," shouted Krogna, before kicking the large green once more. Anger rising higher "Mok ta-booplu, faryoup." The folds on his face tightening with anger.

Boon sighed with relief, pressing the green button until it turned dark once more. Then he pressed an amber button near the green instead. It lit up brightly, lighting the small interior of his pod. He cleared his throat.

"You . . . hear . . . me?"

Krogna smiled before pressing his own amber button. "Yes, you speak Earthling. Question is, you understand it?"

Boon nodded. "Yes"

"Good, good." Krogna pulled out a data pad and began tapping symbols with three long slender fingers until the screen flashed red. "You know procedure, yes?"

"Yes," Boon grunted.

Krogna pressed a button inside the interior and suddenly, dozens of large rope membranes came from holes on the sides, wrapping around Boon, steadying him upright, tightly. A soft, large metallic hose hovered over the green, and wavered above his lips before pushing forward and down his throat, which he accepted. A yellow looking substance slowly began filling his lungs.

"Good luck, friend," Krogna said, and pressed another button, shutting and sealing the pod's doors. He punched a code from the outside, then looked through a small window where he watched the interior fill up with thick red gel. Moments later a deep noise rattled throughout the ship. The pod slid from its cradle, suction pulled the tear shaped craft through a tunnel carved deep within. The pod followed its path, picking up speed before being shot into space, toward that always debatable lonely blue and green gem known as Earth.

Even with his lungs filled with breathable liquid and surrounded by cold, shock absorbing gel, Boon was going to be conscious for the duration of the short trip.

The journey from the Maerrisian Battleship to Earth would be fairly simple. The Battleship itself was in sync with its surroundings-creating perfect cloaking. Earthlings were probably another century away from figuring out they had been watched by such a vessel for centuries. But, by then, it would be too late.

The pod, which was only a few meters larger than Boon himself, would look like a falling star, a purple one in fact. The impact had been planned to be a dry landing, and far from enjoyable. Impacting the Earth at around five hundred miles per hour. At its peak speed, the pod would travel close to seventeen hundred, but thrusters would kick in a mile out, and hopefully the gel would be bound properly by the time impact occurred. The pod was designed to hit at its point, where large fibre-like tentacles would harpoon out and grasp objects, preventing the craft from lodging too far into whatever lay below. The drop-pod started to rock heavily, and Boon went over the basics of the plan to settle his nerves.

The Maerrisian's had decided to keep watch over the ever advancing Earth for nearly six hundred years, and had recently discovered that conflicts on the pretty planet were not going so well. Intelligence was gathering hard facts over eighteen Earth months, and as much as everyone wanted to dismiss it, governments were well on their way to beginning what they would call 'World War III'. The council agreed this would not be allowed. Losing humanity was acceptable, but the Earth itself was one of a kind. The human weapons were advancing far too fast, and another World War would only advance this further. Today a decision would be made. Should the planet itself be saved now?

Other species over the decades had tried communicating with humanity, but everything so far had been swiftly swatted by governments. The Maerrisian were a different matter for the humans, for they were the first, and they had created The Outer Rim Alliance. What they decided, all others followed. His initial objective was to make first contact. From there, word was to spread so that, in time, talking to the governments would be possible, but only after word had gotten out to enough people. If this objective was compromised, he was to make contact with the Battleship where Maerrisian Cruisers were waiting in deep space to play their role, a more sinister one, for humans. The planet would benefit much more if it came to the later, Boon figured.

The pod shot through the atmosphere with a purple trail arcing behind it. The thrusters engaged one mile out, and the red and orange membrane tentacles homed in on everything surrounding the landing site, attaching to trees, rocks, a scarecrow, and dozens of other structures. The pod kissed the Earth. Dirt, rocks, and parts of a tree sprang hundreds of meters into the air.

Silence slowly returned to the land, which was mostly in darkness. Fingers of orange and purple crept across the horizon from the east. Roosters in the distance announcing the awakening of a new day.

Time passed, and the first rays of light brushed upon the ivory colored pod. A small, soft click came and steam poured forth. A door popped out slightly, and red ooze gushed out from within. Moments later, another hiss and the door slid completely open, light penetrating the interior, dampening the purple and blue flashing lights.

Boon leaped out, hunching, whist covering his eyes, protecting them from the sudden glare. He felt the red ooze on his body crystallize as the sunlight washed over him, which he dusted off. He heard a chirp, most likely a bird, and then stood up straight, rising to his full height of fifteen feet. He stretched out the aches that had spread throughout his one ton frame, all ripping muscle.

He started walking, but stopped. "Stupid!"

He backtracked to the craft, reached inside, and grabbed a large object. A massive, dull ebony and silver sword, which was ten feet long with a blade that, at the base, was six inches thick. It was big, and it was for the strong bad ass and unbreakable-unlike those it chose to greet. He slipped it into the holster over his back, where it hung diagonally.

Boon licked his lips and spat on his green grubby hands. He wiped them over two, large black ridged horns rising out just above his forehead, and twisting back over his head. They gleamed slightly. It was a sign of respect to keep your horns wet and gleaming.

On his left arm, Boon had a touch-screen-data-pad. The information told him he was five human miles away from the nearest town-a small village by the looks of it, with few people. This, he thought, was a good start.

Just a few miles into the trek, he stopped and wiped sweat from his forehead. It was running down his back in large globs. Earth was much cooler than his home world, but the gravity was heavier. It could have been due to ten years planted on that stinking observation battleship, now that he thought about it. How he hoped this mission wouldn't take long.

Nearing a small town, a tiny amber dot appeared on the screen. Someone neared by. This was it.

Around him hundreds of colorful trees stood only slightly taller than his huge frame. They were full of round berries, or seeds, or maybe fruit. Human ecology was a weak point, which he cared little for. Boon liked meat, greasy meat, and full of dripping fat.

The monitor said the human was only twenty meters away. He walked toward a much larger tree so he could hide behind for cover. No colorful round objects hung from its branches, just lots of shade. He hid behind it, or as much as a one ton, fifteen foot alien that looked half human and half bull could.

Peering around the trunk, he was somewhat bemused. The human was small. It was very small, Boon thought it had to be a child or some weakling. He really wished he had Krogna's brain, or had at least paid attention in class.

The child was sitting on the ground playing with some toys that were made in the image of a human. The child was too busy to notice anything else. It was talking to the toys in a high-pitched voice, and then talking back in a deeper one. Were humans really this odd? It looked so strange. Long, curly black locks hung to its shoulders. It had fluffy pink cheeks, huge blue eyes, and it must like meat as well, because Boon could see it had many teeth missing. It was wearing a white sleeveless dress with blue flowers. The mud on the ground had stained its knees and dress.

If he wanted to complete the mission, he had to find an elder. He stepped around the tree, slowly walking so the little human would not look up from its activity. Underfoot a thick fallen tree branch snapped beneath Boon's left foot. "Great," he muttered under his breath.

The little one saw him. He was sure it would run off screaming. This was not going to plan.

The child looked at its two toy Earthlings and said, "Look, look, another friend for your wedding." It placed the toys in the mud, got up clumsily, and rushed toward Boon with an odd looking expression. A smile.

This was unexpected, he thought.

The little one walked up to him, in his shadow, standing not much taller than his knee. It bent its neck back, and the child's blue eyes stared deep into his own.

"Wowwy, you sure are big," it said as it cocked its head to the side, "and green."

Boon wriggled his snout and snorted. It smelt . . . off.

The child laughed, whilst covering its mouth.

"Will you come to their wedding?" it asked, pointing to the lifeless toys laying face down in the mud. "Please, please, please?"

Boon turned his head, hoping maybe the child would get bored. It walked around until it was in his vision again, than waved.

It covered its eyes, blocking the bright morning sun. "Hello."

"Human."

It laughed again. "You talk funny."

He snorted again. "You look stupid, and smell strange."

The child placed its hand on its hips and frowned. "How rude," then it laughed. "Mummy would think so. She always says that to daddy, but he's not, daddy's funny."

"I must talk to an Elder, child. Important."

The child's smile fell away before it pulled something out of a pocket in the dress. It was round and pink. He had seen them on the trees.

"At least have an apple; they're super yummy, double even." It stretched an arm out which still didn't reach his waist. "Just don't eat too many. Your tummy will hurt." It strained on its tippy-toes and thrust the apple toward him, until it was making strange gasping sounds.

He sighed, bent down, and with his finger tips, grasped the small apple from its hand.

"Try it, try it."

He placed it in his mouth and barely tasted anything. So small it could have got stuck between his teeth. He thought he tasted something sweet, maybe.

"Will you be my friend?" the child suddenly asked.

He snorted as he often did when confused. "Sure, but . . . "

The child placed a hand around one of his fingers, or tried to, and then tried to pull him over to the toys. "Come on, just for a while. Please, please."

They sat for almost an hour. Apparently the white doll, named Lisa, was marrying the ebony doll, Gregory. After the wedding, he sat and pretended to drink champagne out of a white plastic teacup. The girl child told him how Mummy was always nagging Daddy, and making him mad. She told him how Daddy was always working, and she told him how a boy called Dale had kissed her behind the barn last week on her sixth birthday. It was gross apparently.

"Mary," a voice called out in the distance. "Mary, where are you?" It sounded worried.

"Mummy," the girl cried out in response. She grabbed his finger again. "Come, let's go talk to the adults now."

"You are sure?"

She nodded. "Hurry though, Mummy hates waiting."

Together they got up. She handed him Lisa and Gregory while she wiped dirt off her skirt and knees. "Follow me." She kept a hold of his finger and tried to skip along.

They reached the end of the line of trees, coming to a field which was open. A hundred yards away a small white house, in between stood some bigger humans. Perfect, Boon thought, Elders.

Mary ran toward her mother. "Mummy, Mummy. Look at my new friend . . . "

Mary's mother screamed. "Mary, get over here now, get over here." She ran toward the child, grabbing her arm. She let out another blood curdling scream when she saw how close she was to it.

"A monster!" she screamed. "Martin, get the gun! Now! Fast! Hurry!" Her words were a blur in the haste of panic.

She dragged Mary by the arm and ran. Mary cried with pain. "Mummy he's my friend," she said. "Ouch! Mummy, that hurts. Mummy!"

The child's mother let go of her arm and looked down with a snarl. She swung her hand, slapping her daughter hard across the face. It sounded like the large branch Boon had snapped under his foot earlier "How dare you? How dare you be so reckless?"

A bunch of men came running out; all holding what Boon figured were weapons. He looked at Mary, crying with a large red hand print on her face.

How could this have gone wrong so quickly?

"What the hell is that?" screamed one man with a strange straw hat on.

"Oh my god!" screamed another while pulling out a few cartridges for the shotgun.

"Good Lord, what the hell?" exclaimed the last of the three men; a smoke hanging between his lips.

"Shoot it, shoot it," pleaded the woman. "For God sake."

Boon stepped forward. "Please humans, we talk . . ."

They either didn't hear, or didn't care. The three men aimed their guns toward the green creature and pulled their triggers. He was shot in the chest, legs, and arms. None of the shots were critical, or even close to being so. One thing Maerrisian's had was muscle, and tough skin. As weak as the bullets may have been though, dark blue blood

109

dribbled down from his wounds where the bullets lodged. Another round of shots came his way with more hitting; one in the mouth. It hurt. His body started to feel itchy, sore even. He didn't like this. Nobody was listening to him or wanted too.

"Leave him alone!" cried Mary. She dropped Lisa and Gregory and ran toward her new friend. She ran as fast as her little legs would allow her.

The girl had only crossed half the distance between the two before her body twisted in funny directions. Her mouth opening up before a scream escaped. She fell awkwardly to the ground.

The mother screamed as well, but silenced when the monster rushed toward her daughter, picking her up. "Leave my daughter alone, you beast!" she roared.

Boon looked at the girl who was on her back, sobbing. Her white dress with the delicate blue flower pattern, now blooming red buds as well. He bent down, picking her up, watching the buds turn into rose petals. He ignored the older human' cries and ran back toward the line of trees as fast as he could, with the child cradled on his arm. He had to cover some distance, and fast.

Every once in awhile, he looked down at the child to make sure she was still breathing. After ten or so minutes of flat out running he had left the humans well and truly behind. He stopped, sat down, and lifted his hands to get a closer look of his friend, Mary.

The red petals that had appeared were now one giant flower on Mary's chest. It had spread out with ribbons of crimson, now running down her left arm, and out the corner of her mouth. She coughed and the flow became stronger.

"Mummy," she whispered, then shook her head. "No, it's you." Her eyes swam in happiness.

Boon snorted. "It's me, Boon, your friend."

The girl tried to smile. "You'll be my friend always, won't you?"

Boon felt an odd pain in his chest. "Forever and ever, little human." It felt so tight, so hard to breathe.

Something inside his chest ached and his eyes stung. He didn't know what was wrong, but he couldn't stop snorting. He had never felt a pain like this in his entire life.

He wanted to say more, but when he looked down, the girl's arm fell off his hand, limply. Her eyes open, but lifeless. Boon knew she was dead.

He placed her on the ground gently before punching the nearest tree as hard as he could, almost tearing it from the earth, letting out a deafening roar of anger. Birds in the distance took flight, unhappy to be startled.

Time passed. He wasn't sure how long, but the sun rose well over his head and started to lower again on the other side. His mind felt numb. He no longer knew what to do. He wanted humans to suffer so badly, but allowing this would mean girls like Mary would never have the chance to live. He stroked Mary's cold cheek. "Someone else's decision. No longer Boon's."

He waited until he heard voices. It was dark now and he could just make out light flashing through the distant trees. He no longer cared. As horrid as humans were, they had given him something, anger, rage. He didn't care anymore. Life felt different. Meanings no longer the same.

He walked toward the tree where abeam finally struck him. "Over there, OVER THERE!" A loud machine rattling noise exploded around him, dozens of them, followed by pain all over. He ran near a cluster of lights, stomping until they went away and voices screamed in agony.

There was nothing more he could do. More lights came forth, dozens and dozens, so many voices, so much hate. He didn't care though, it was surprising he thought. He sank to his knees as hundreds of bullets penetrated his skin, and eventually deeper within. His vision became dark. The world became silent. He fell forward from his knees, onto the earth. For a second, he heard cheers of victory around him. His last thought was what everything intelligent, and stupid alike, in the universe thinks at some point in their life. Why?

Somewhere in the lands we all shall come to know one day, a human girl named Mary, and a Maerrisian known as Boon, danced in God's embrace as one, where they were friends forever and ever.

IN HER EYES, THE SKIES
BY J. RODIMUS FOWLER

It always starts the same, my dream that is, and it's always the same. It's a vicious circle that ends the same way every time. I am always driving off into the night, always running from her, even though I have never met her, not in the flesh, anyway. I think that I remember a time before the dream, but I can't be sure, my mind's been a little uncooperative as of late. In fact, I now know that I am crazy. Let me rephrase that, I am shit-house crazy…or am I?

At first I tried to tell people, but no one ever listened to me. They treated me as if I were one of those dreary old men on the street corner holding up a cardboard sign that read, *The end is near* or *Judgment day is coming*. They should have listened to me, but I must have looked intolerable. My clothes were a mess and I hadn't shaved in a long while, or showered for that matter, so I was probably a little repugnant as well. We are all ignorant sometimes, who could blame them? I must have come off like a madman, at the very least a raving lunatic. After all, I was 'Chicken Little' the adult version, with swear words and all. I told them that she was coming and with her came the skies.

I had been dreaming of her for as long as I could remember, but once again, I'm not thinking straight. I had known her face my whole adult life or maybe even before. I was always on the lookout for her, trying to find her first. Like a needle in a stack of humans, she was fleeting. I warned everyone that I met of the dangers she would bring. She rode no pale horse, but Death followed her just the same, like a loyal little puppy trotting by her side.

* * *

I passed her on the side of the highway just outside of Houston or maybe it was in a dream. I was speeding down the road in my blood-red Cadillac El Dorado doing about ninety miles an hour when I saw her standing there. She was a thing of rare beauty standing in the middle of a ghost town, which was usually heavily populated. I looked back in my rear view mirror and saw her start to walk down

113

the road behind me in the same direction. I swear there were bright white clouds in the sky the whole day, and there still were ahead of me, but the skies to my rear were empty, dull and pale. It wasn't like there was a storm coming. It was like the skies had lost their flair, lost their life, leaving only a blank canvas behind.

I pushed the accelerator to the floor until I arrived at the next town. It was called Fox Hollow and it was full of busy bodies going on with their daily routines. I stopped and told them to flee. I told them that she was coming this way, but like everyone else I ever told, they just ignored me. That is, until someone came from one of the shops and started shouting that they had lost communications with any place north of their location. Everyone started whipping out their cell phones, people flooded 911 with the land lines, which soon became a constant busy signal. Even the satellite and cable signals for the television turned to static.

More and more people were driven from their homes in search of knowledge. They wanted to know what was going on, why were their electronic devices on the fritz. Some of the business owners left their stores unattended and gathered on the sidewalks asking questions, for which I had the only answers. I tried to tell them that she was coming and that she was crying. She was always crying in my dreams. The masses just thought that I was crazy and that the mishap was a freak communication break-down.

I needed to get prepared or at least calm my nerves so I walked into the 'The Swamp' a nice little tavern about a block away from where I had parked the old Caddy. I poured myself three shots of tequila straight up, no training wheels for me. I was versed well in the ways of tequila. I drank down all three of the shots one after the other and swished the last shot around in my mouth for a couple of seconds to savor the magnificent taste. I left a fifty dollar bill on the bar because the tender was outside with everyone else, some of which had stopped in their tracks to stare at the cloudless skies.

I walked back outside and sat down on a bench out front of the tavern. It was only 3:17pm, but darkness was fast on its way from the north. I could hear the gossip and rumors spreading through the scared citizens. One man said it was a government experiment because they always did those kinds of tests on small towns like this one. Another man blamed terrorists with some new kind of weapon or device. An old lady started to scream aliens! I had to agree with the latter, the crying woman was definitely not of this Earth, but she was on her way.

At first it looked like the stars to the north were just burning out. I mean they glowed brighter than ever for just a second, kind of like they were getting closer, then nothing. They just disappeared one at a time. The dull darkness of the sky looked like it was closing in on the town, like you could reach out and touch it if you were tall enough. Then it happened, right in front of everyone, the moon disappeared. It simply vanished.

A man wearing a bright orange hunter's cap let out a scream that could have awakened the dead. I jumped to my feet and we all stared his way as he floated up into the air just above our heads. He screamed again, but it was cut short as his skin closed in on itself, he looked instantly dehydrated. He turned into dust and blew away. Flesh, bone and hair alike, all withered in a matter of milliseconds.

An uproar of cries spread throughout the crowd as they panicked and scattered in every direction. The young trampling over the old, the fast over the slow, it was mass chaos. All above their heads, people were floating up and turning to dust.

The old lady from before shouted out as she was floating, "Aliens!"

I got up and ran to my Cadillac blood mobile, jumped in without opening the door and started the engine. I peeled out burning rubber down the asphalt as fast as my El Dorado would take me. As I peered back into my mirrors I saw the rest of the townspeople blow away in one big dust cloud. Even the few that had made it to their cars and were chasing behind me, were sucked out their windows and carried away with the wind, leaving their cars coasting to a halt. I looked back once more and saw her coming. She was walking straight down the middle of the road, straight toward me and I could tell she was still crying. I put the pedal to the metal and held on tight.

I drove as fast as I could for about ten miles, watching the stars disappear behind me in my mirrors. I saw the daylight way ahead of me and I saw the darkness right behind. I thought of all the people waiting ahead of me at the next town and how I wouldn't be able to save them either, how they would never believe me. Then my thoughts drifted to her face, her crying eyes and the loneliness there in.

She had captured my soul, but maybe that's what she does. Maybe she just travels the universe alone, from one planet to another, taking everything she wants like some sort of lonely God. Maybe she just wants some company to share the world with, maybe she just wants me.

I suddenly had a change of heart. I slammed on the brakes and slung the blood-mobile around. I would run no more. I drove toward the crying woman and stopped my Cadillac about a hundred yards in front of her, leaving the headlights shining bright. They were two beams of light cutting through the swirling darkness ahead. I could see the road behind her turning brown, to ash and dust. I could see the grass cracking just before it blew away. The air, itself was dissipating. It was getting hard to breathe. I stepped out of the Caddy and started walking to her, and she to me.

When we were close enough, we said at exactly the same time, "I dreamed of you."

We reached out and grabbed each other in a loving embrace. I kissed her and she kissed me back, the most passionate kiss of all time. The whole world stopped and I could see in her eyes. I saw the missing stars and all the missing people. I saw the Heavens and I saw the hells, the living and the dead. I could see in her eyes…the skies. She was my lost Messiah and I, her disciple. Together we would make a new world, a better world, a world of complete bliss.

* * *

I awoke this morning to the sounds of my alarm clock radio. I stood up and looked out my window at my pearl white Cadillac El Dorado. I decided that instant to paint it blood-red today, after all I had already bought the paint. There was something on the morning news about a loss of communication with Canada. People were even talking about some of the northern stars were no longer visible, like they had just disappeared. I still have a little time and I know what she wants now. It's what we all want, love…true love. That is, unless my dream is wrong.

AXES TO AXES, DUST TO DUST
BY J. RODIMUS FOWLER

My name is Richard Hutchins and I used to be a fireman. Used to be, is the correct wording because now when there is a fire we just watch from our boarded up windows. The aliens stand around laughing and snorting, watching the fires burn, grabbing any unlucky soul that they could catch and roasting them on the fire.

These things were huge, some of them ten feet tall and they had enormous feet and hands. Their mouths were not small either, big enough to eat a man whole and pick their teeth with his bones. Our leg bones were just right for that. They resembled large gorillas with the heads of wide-mouthed frogs with two sharp fangs protruding up from their lower mandibles. Their skin was reptile like and scaly with a dull grey color. They also had webbed feet with a particular grizzly looking set of claws on the end.

No one knows exactly where they came from. We all kind of agreed that it was outer space. They just came walking up one day, with no flying saucers and no space ships. Now we have to stay in-doors almost all of the time, which makes it hard to even get bread and milk these days, let alone some good whiskey.

Just yesterday, Tim Hobolder was on the way to get some grocer-ies when he was scooped up by one of the things in a most painful way. The alien pulled Tim's hands behind his back so hard that it dis-located one of his shoulders, and then it drug him around the corner behind the Post Office. After a few minutes of silence we heard screaming, violent uncontrollable screaming, then we heard silence again. Only the thing came back from behind the store. The bastard was laughing whole heartedly.

I had been watching from my windows and so had Tony Leone. He was my neighbor and part of Squad 13. Tony and I lived beside each other and Von lived across town, we could see his roof from our houses. That was us, well almost, we were Squad 13 the Honeycutt, Georgia volunteer Fire Department.

Jerry "The Axe" Mahoney was our squad leader and I wished he was here. He had gone on vacation two weeks ago and was supposed to be back last Tuesday. The aliens had shown up in his stead. He was

117

clear headed during complete chaos, and this was an exacting chaos. He was the best axe man I had ever seen. Now I'll admit that I'm no slouch with an axe and neither are my guys, but we were one man short, our leader.

Von was very sneaky and tried shooting them at first. Their skin would just absorb the bullets with no harm. Some of the other towns-people tried Molotov cocktails, but the aliens were resilient. It just made them go on a rampage, violently striking out against the nearest person. All of the townspeople learned to stay locked up in their homes unless necessity took over. The aliens slept outside in the middle of town so they could catch anyone that they saw trying to leave. Those that tried got it the worst. They were toasted, ate and bone-picked. We learned fast 'out of sight, out of mind.'

The aliens quickly learned who ran the shops, and replaced the necessary dead. They knew to keep the vital shops open so their food source, us, would stay ripe for the picking. Our friend Gregory was forced to take over the grocery store.

Last night Tony and I went on a supply run to see Gregory. We carried our axes with us just in case. We left under the cloak of night. We made our way, hiding from time to time, but we arrived at the back door. There was a ladder that led up to the roof and there was a hatch that led down into the store. We made it inside with no problem until we saw the look on Gregory's face.

One of the aliens was standing right beside us. I noticed it was missing its left hand. It leapt out quickly, but not quick enough. I hit it square in the mouth with my axe, sinking it so deep into its skull that it got stuck. Tony followed my action and chopped off the things right hand. I put my boot on the alien's forehead and had to jerk with all my might just to get my axe free. Then we cut off all of the alien's limbs, even his frog shaped head.

It worked, tearing them to pieces, actually killed them. These bas-tards were mortal after all. "Axes to axes, dust to dust," Tony said. We just looked at each other and smiled.

This morning, when the aliens found the pieces of their dismem-bered friend, they immediately went on a rampage. Gregory was the first to get caught. He screamed as one of the creatures slammed him to the ground hard enough to kill him.

They grabbed everyone they saw, even breaking down doors and snatching people from their homes. They piled up the bodies in the middle of the road in the center of town. Tony came straight to my house and we called Von up on the county issued walkie-talkies and told him the plan. Since Jerry was gone, that made me the next in command. It was time to fight or die trying.

We suited up in our protective firemen's gear, boots, coats and helmets. We walked right out my front door toward the center of town. I walked with my axe slung over my shoulder. Tony held his with both hands, ready to strike.

The first alien to see us came running our way. As soon as he was in reach, Tony swung his axe like the mighty Babe Ruth. He made contact, splitting the creature's mouth even wider with his deadly face shot. I followed that blow up by taking each of the alien's hands and feet.

In half the blink of an eye another creature was on top of us. It slapped Tony across the back with its large hands, knocking him to the ground. I slammed my axe down into the thing's foot, cutting right through it.

Then from out of nowhere Von was on the creature, like ink on paper. He had a machete in each hand and struck the alien on each side of the neck in a 'V' shaped pattern, sending its head rolling along the asphalt right up to Tony. Tony got up and kicked the head down the street catching the attention of two more creatures.

They stood their ground and we stood ours, no one making the first move. Then we heard the sound of steel being drug against asphalt. The sound even caught the aliens by surprise. They just stared past us. We turned our backs to the creatures and saw the silhouette of a man dragging an axe behind him along the road.

It was Jerry "The Axe" Mahoney, in full fireman's gear. His yellow coat was now crimson and his face was covered in blood. He said, "All right, let's get these frog-looking mother fuckers...Squad 13 Honeycutt, Georgia. Its axe time, boys!"

Then we took his lead, gripped our axes tight and started walking toward the creatures. The aliens actually looked scared, scared of a group of volunteer firefighters with no fires to fight, but a fight we would bring!

For the next hour or so, the middle of town square sounded like steel cutting flesh, and flesh hitting stone. All of the people left their hiding spots and came outside to watch. As soon as we, the squad, had killed the last of the aliens left roaming around we stopped to catch our breath. Jerry, Tony, Von and I raised our axes and touched them in the air, just like a high five for blades.

All of the town's folk that were left gathered around to thank us. Jerry spoke up and said, "Who wants to take Gregory's place? We need a new grocery store attendant."

I looked over at Jerry and said, "Is it time my friend?"

He simply nodded.

The rest of the Squad and I reached up and pulled our fake faces off revealing our true selves. Our dog-like faces scared the shit out of the townspeople, but at least we weren't as scary as the creatures that we had just taken care of. Who would have guessed that the Volunteer Fire Department Squad 13 Honeycutt, Georgia were a bunch of dog-faced freaks? Dogs mark their territory, and we had marked ours. The aliens should have known that, but in the end, they were kind of stupid.

THE LOST
BY R. W. HAWKINS

The soldiers aimed their rifles at the family huddled on the floor. The television blared static and nonsense. The lights were flickering. Two corpses were on the floor, and an injured man was on the sofa. The stink of blood and ruptured flesh hung in the air like a bad joke. Gunfire crackled in the street outside.

Lewis held his wife and his daughter. There was blood on his shirt. Hysteria lurked somewhere in his mind, ignored because he would be dead in a few seconds. The high-powered automatic rifles, at such a short range, would turn them into crimson memories against the wall.

He gave his family a tired, sad smile. "Close your eyes."

Three hours earlier...

Dusk was falling when the news bulletin came on the television.

Lewis and his wife, Emily, were sitting on the sofa, her legs laid over his lap as she marked her students' test papers with a red pen. He was drinking a beer.

"Your feet smell," Lewis said.

"No, they don't," replied Emily, softly elbowing him in the ribs. "I had a shower earlier."

Lewis covered his nose. "That's some quality cheese we got here."

"Sod off, Lew; you're the one with the stinky feet."

Lewis uncovered his nose and laughed, waving his hand in front of his face. Emily returned to her papers, grinning. Lewis watched Sara sitting cross-legged on the carpet, playing with her Dora the Explorer toys. He couldn't help but smile at her, their little girl; their firstborn. She had her mother's eyes, big and wide and always questioning. The way her face screwed up when she was puzzled could make him laugh until his nose bled.

The football match between England and Spain vanished from the television screen, and the BBC news came on. The news anchor was pale, and his eyes were a little too wide, as if he was on a bad acid trip. Lewis recognised him but didn't know his name.

Emily looked up from her papers, her pen dangling over misspelled words. "What happened to the football?"

Lewis didn't answer; he was listening to the television. Sara kept playing with her toys.

The news anchor's voice was even and measured despite his outward appearance. "Sorry for the interruption...This is a special bulletin..." He took a deep breath. "There are confirmed reports of giant 'objects' in the skies over Britain and the rest of the world." He paused, as if to let those words sink in. "This is not a hoax, this is real. At 7:57 PM, the first UFOs appeared over Britain, the same moment as they appeared over other countries. At the moment they are stationary. I repeat: this is not a hoax." The man was sweating. "Now, over to Jane Marlow, reporting live from just outside Oxford, where one of the...UFOs has been sighted. Jane, what is happening there?"

"That's not too far from us," said Emily, her voice low.

Lewis leaned forward. Emily was right; their village was a whisper north of the M4 motorway, about thirty miles from Oxford. Not too far at all.

His testicles crawled up into his body.

Jane Marlow appeared, standing in a field. People were behind her, looking up at the sky. She was a sharp-faced, red-haired woman.

"Thanks, Bill. I'm here, just outside of Oxford. This is incredible, Bill. The UFO is hovering in the sky at an estimated height of four thousand feet. We don't know where it or the others came from. Are they man-made? It's a mystery at the moment."

The camera panned high above her to show the UFO; dark and ugly, crudely-shaped like a pile of metal fused together. A single yellow light blinked on its side.

"There's been no official statement from the government...or any government yet," Bill's voice asked.

"That's correct, Bill."

"We've already had people saying that aliens have arrived. Is this possible, Jane, or just a joke?"

"Well, Bill, that seems to be the popular opinion at the moment. As far as we know, no country on Earth has this kind of technology...Look at the size of it; it's bigger than any aircraft. And it's also stationary...so unless it and the others are some kind of secret prototype craft, then the alien theory is very, very plausible."

"Are we talking about First Contact, Jane?"

"It's impossible to confirm it at the moment. Like you said, there's been no statement from the government yet. All we can do is wait."

"And the important thing to do is not to panic," said Bill.

"Absolutely, Bill."

"Thank you, Jane." The camera returned to the studio. "I've just had confirmation that the Prime Minister is about to address the nation from Ten Downing Street. We'll go straight there in a few minutes."

Lewis noticed Bill's hands shaking slightly.

He looked at Emily. She had tears in her eyes. The test papers were on the floor. Lewis downed the rest of the beer, wishing he had some stronger stuff in the house. This was unreal, this was surreal...this was impossible.

Sara turned to them, forgetting her toys. "Is this the end of the world?"

Emily held out her arms for Sara; the girl jumped onto her mother's lap with such ease it was if the shapes of their bodies were shaped for each other.

"No, Sara," Emily said. "Everything's gonna be okay. What gave you such a silly idea?"

Sara pressed her head to her mother's chest. "You and Daddy look scared..."

Lewis exchanged a look with Emily. He said to Sara, "Nothing bad's going to happen, darling. Everything's going to be fine."

It was getting dark outside.

They turned back to the television. Bill was listening to the producer through his earpiece. His throat worked as he swallowed; beads of sweat on his forehead. "Um, something's happened..." He was listening to the producer again. "Okay...we're going back to Jane Marlow...there's been a development..."

The screen went black for a second, then Jane Marlow appeared. The people behind her were still staring at the sky. One man had covered his ears. Jane was speaking, but she couldn't be heard above the roar of jet engines. She shook her head and pointed upwards; the cameraman caught on and turned the camera to the sky.

A column of white lights had activated on the side of the UFO.

Fighter jets screamed into view. Missiles were launched, striking the craft. The UFO started to move as the jets swarmed around it. Another missile found its mark and smoke poured from all sides. Its flight path was erratic, limping across the darkening sky.

Vapour trails raked the sky. Two more missiles found their target; part of the craft exploded in a bright, flaming light.

"Oh my god," said Emily. "Are we really seeing this?"

Lewis said nothing. Sara was crying, sucking her thumb.

The jets circled the UFO; they had run out of missiles. But it didn't matter; it was going down. Lewis could hear Jane's voice shouting something as the craft began to descend.

Then several parts of the ship broke away from the main body, falling to Earth. Jane was shouting again. The other people were screaming; the shrillness of their cries made his hair stand on end.

The screen went dark as if someone had thrown a blanket over the camera.

Silence.

"Oh, for fuck's sake," said Lewis. Emily didn't scold him for swearing, as she usually would; she was staring, open-mouthed at the television. He waited for the picture to return; when it didn't he tried the other channels but found them all dark.

Lewis turned to the television. He stood in the center of the living room, sweat coating the flaws and creases of his body. His mouth tasted of sour beer and bad food.

"It's going to be OK," Emily told Sara.

Lewis went to the window, looked outside. The street was empty. He thought about alien invasions, and all the films he had seen about them. In most films, villages were never attacked; it was always the cities that were destroyed.

"We should be safe," he whispered.

There was a distant roar. Lewis looked at the sky. His mouth fell open.

"Emily, come and see this."

"What's wrong?"

"Just come here."

She joined him at the window, Sara in her arms, who had retreated into a dazed sleep.

Something was falling across the sky, toward the ground like a meteor. It disappeared behind the houses on the other side of the street; there was a distant thump. A plume of smoke rose seconds later. It had landed a few miles outside the village.

"What's happening?" asked Emily. "What are we going to do?"

Lewis was still staring at the trail the object had left across the sky. "We're going to lock the doors and stay in the house."

* * *

Ten minutes later, there was a knock on the front door. Lewis looked out the window. Danny Willard's Toyota was parked by the pavement.

Lewis unlocked and opened the front door. Danny was grinning like an insurance agent; behind him were Lewis's other mates, Tom and Roy Bunting, two brothers. They had all been in the same class at school, apart from Roy who was a year younger. Danny was a self-styled ladies' man; it was a shame he was suffering from a receding hairline and a paunch, even in his early thirties. His teeth were perfect, though.

"Lewis, you coming out to play?" Danny said. Tom and Roy nodded at Lewis.

"Evening, lads. What's going on?"

"Don't you know?" Danny said. "Fucking aliens, that's what's going on! Did you see that thing crash a few minutes ago? We're going to see where it landed. You coming?"

"I can't," Lewis said. "I can't leave Emily and Sara here alone. Won't it be a bit dangerous, Danny?"

Danny shook his head, that stupid grin slashed onto his face like a knife-wound. "Don't be such a wimp. Other people from the village are going as well. We're just gonna have a look around, see what we can find. Might be some wreckage...We could sell it. Just think how much alien wreckage will be worth!"

"Yeah," Tom and Roy muttered together.

"It's a bad idea," said Lewis.

"Yeah, yeah," Danny said. "You sound like my mother..."

"Your mother gave up on you long ago. I'm just trying to talk some sense into you, Danny."

"I know you've always been the sensible one, Lewis, but seriously when did you have your testicle-removal operation done? Was it before or after you got married?"

"Very funny. I can't go. I've got a daughter who's in tears and thinks it's the end of the world."

"Just tell her that we won. The jets knocked those ships out of the air. Everything's fine."

Lewis looked over his shoulder, then back at Danny. He sighed.

Danny playfully punched him on the arm. "Listen, mate, you're either coming or you're not...so what're you gonna do? Last chance..."

"I can't, Danny. I've got to stay here."

Danny's grin faltered for a second. "Okay, mate. Your decision." He turned to Tom and Roy. "Let's go, fellas." He shook his head at Lewis. "See ya later, Family Man."

"Wait," said Lewis.

Danny turned around. Lewis motioned for him to come closer.

"What, Lewis?"

"Be careful, Danny Boy," he whispered. "Look after Tom and Roy. They're well-intentioned but they've never been the cleverest. Don't do anything stupid."

Danny grinned again, teeth as white as freshly-made paper. "No worries, mate." He slapped Lewis on the shoulder then sauntered to his car. Tom and Roy followed.

Something cold uncoiled itself inside Lewis as he watched them drive away. He closed the door, locked it and returned to the living room. Emily was pacing the room, her face stretched tight across her bones. She held her mobile phone.

"What's wrong now?" Lewis asked.

"The internet and the house phone are down. Even the network on my mobile is down. I tried to call my sister in Bournemouth."

Lewis took his mobile from his pocket. He tried calling Emily's phone, but he had the same problem.

"Shit." He flicked the light switch, and the bulb sparked into life. "We've still got electricity, though." The coldness inside him started to spread. His mouth had dried up.

Lewis hugged his wife, reassuring her with his eyes. "We'll be fine."

* * *

They huddled on the sofa, Lewis and Emily drinking tea from novelty mugs while Sara slept next to her mother. Lewis found himself staring at Sara's small, porcelain face, the rise and fall of her chest, the way her blonde hair curled around her ears.

"Maybe we should go outside and talk to the neighbours," said Emily.

"I don't know," said Lewis. "I think it's better to stay inside."

"But we have to find out what's happening…"

Lewis looked at her. "Do we really?" He was thinking about Sara; how he couldn't risk anything happening to her. "I say we stay here, wait this out. The news said there were more of those UFOs. We don't know how dangerous it is out there. I used to read stories about aliens invading the Earth when I was a kid. Even then I thought it was bollocks, really."

Emily sipped her tea. "Looks like all of us were wrong…"

"Yeah."

There was a voice coming from outside; it sounded unnatural; distorted and echoic. It was getting louder.

"What the hell is that?" said Lewis.

They left Sara on the sofa, and walked to the window, peeking through the gap in the curtains.

The voice was almost on top of them now. Lewis could hear dogs barking as well.

Caught in the yellow streetlights, soldiers were moving down the street, gas masks on their faces and rifles slung across their bodies. Sniffer dogs strained at their leashes. A humvee cruised between the rows of soldiers, a loudspeaker on its roof, an amplified male voice pouring through it.

"Please stay in your homes. I repeat: please stay in your homes. This is for your own safety. I repeat: please stay in your homes." This was repeated over and over.

Of course, people weren't staying in their homes. Mr. and Mrs. Little from across the street were trying to talk to the soldiers, but they were ushered back indoors. The soldiers' rifles were a powerful deterrent to anyone wishing to argue. From the house next to them, Mark Foley emerged, swearing and throwing his arms around; but when the rifles were pointed at him, the fight left him and he retreated toward his front door, hurrying inside.

"Glorious democracy," Lewis muttered as a helicopter buzzed overhead, scanning a searchlight over the village. "Why are they wearing masks? Are they worried about catching something? Are we in danger of catching something?"

Emily's face was as pale as a mound of bleached bones. "They're searching for something, Lewis."

* * *

Darkness had fallen. The curtains had been drawn. Sara was awake, curled up next to Emily, her eyes large and glassy. Lewis imagined everyone else in the village holed up in their homes, scared and confused like them.

The sound of dogs barking in the distance. There had been a flurry of gunshots earlier. It had made Sara cry, but Emily had calmed her down. Lewis watched his daughter tremble on the sofa, feeling powerless to do anything to help her.

"What's going on out there?" Emily asked, just as a jet roared over the house.

Lewis stopped pacing the room. His head throbbed. "Maybe they caught whatever it is they're looking for. Maybe they've shot it."

"I hope so," she said, stroking Sara's hair.

Something banged against the back door. They froze. Sara whimpered. Lewis put a finger to his lips and grabbed a poker from the cold fireplace. He waited. There was a knock at the door, a ragged series of thuds. Lewis went to leave the front room, but Emily shook her head at him. He raised his hand to tell her it was fine. The knocking continued; it was weak but hurried.

Lewis walked down the hallway to the back door. He stopped, and the knocking stopped with him. He listened, leaning his head toward the door. Only silence now.

"Who is it? What do you want?"

"Lewis…"

"Who are you? What are you doing in my back garden?"

"Lewis…it's me…Danny…" Ragged breaths and wet sounds. "Let me in…you twat."

It was definitely Danny out there. Lewis opened the door to reveal his friend leaning against the wall, pale and breathless, blood on his face and his shirt. His left thigh was cut, blood soaking his trousers.

"Oh god, Danny..."

"Don't just stand there," Danny wheezed. "Fucking let me in." His usual grin was an imagined memory.

Lewis dropped the poker, took hold of his mate and guided him through the doorway, just as another helicopter flew overhead, its searchlight flashing across the garden. Danny was soaked with sweat. Lewis shut the door and took Danny to the living room; Emily and Sara gasped when they saw him. They sat him down on the sofa, as gently as they could.

Sara had backed against the wall, her mouth open, hands held to her chest. Lewis wanted to comfort her, but he had to help Danny.

Emily checked Danny's wound. "What happened to your leg?"

"Cut myself on a barbed wire fence," Danny muttered. He looked like he might throw up. Exhaustion was in his face, like it had seeped into his bones. He was trembling, his chest moving too fast to be a good sign.

Lewis looked at his friend, and couldn't find any words.

"Lucky you didn't come with us," said Danny.

"Yeah," Lewis murmured.

And off in the distance was more gunfire.

* * *

Emily cleaned and dressed Danny's wound. The bleeding stopped and she gave him some painkillers. The cut wasn't too deep, had missed any arteries or veins. There was the threat of tetanus, but there were more pressing matters.

Lewis sat down next to Danny. "What happened out there? Where's Roy and Tom?"

Danny offered him a pained grimace, sitting back against the sofa. "Tom and Roy are dead. This is Roy's blood on me. The soldiers did it...We got to the crash site, me, Roy, Tom and some others from the village – there was some kind of...escape pod there, right in the middle of a field, sticking out of the ground. Less than three miles from here. The soldiers came out of nowhere, trying to round us up and put us into trucks. They pointed their guns at us, saying we shouldn't be there, breaking the law...a danger of infection..."

Lewis wondered if that was true about the infection, and if Danny had carried it back with him.

"People were trying to run away. That's when the soldiers started shooting. Roy and Tom were running with me. Tom was shot. "

Emily was shaking her head and cuddling Sara. They both looked like frightened animals, hiding in a hole.

Danny paused, regaining his breath, his body shaking. *Shock*, Lewis thought. They had given him a blanket, tried to keep him warm. They didn't know what else to do.

"Roy and me ran for some woods, trying to get out of the open. Something wet hit me, like rain. It was blood. Then I looked back and he was on the ground. His head was…it was…"

"You're safe now, Danny," said Lewis.

He tried to smile at Lewis, but it would have been a mockery.

"Did you run all the way here?" asked Emily.

"Sort of. Stumbled through the woods. Another patrol saw me, I kept running and cut my leg on barbed wire; hurt like hell."

"It's OK, Danny," Lewis said.

"No, it's not, mate. They've sealed off the village. Something's loose…from that escape pod. It's in the village."

Lewis and Emily looked at each other. He was tempted to say, *Glad we stayed in, now?* to her, but resisted.

There was nothing to do but wait.

* * *

So they waited. Sara had withdrawn into herself. Lewis was afraid she'd become catatonic if things got much worse. Her eyes darted around the room whenever a noise came from outside, and she clung to Emily like a baby monkey to its mother.

Lewis got up from the sofa.

"Where are you going?" Emily's eyes were wide and glassy.

Lewis stretched his arms and groaned. "Just going to check the doors and windows. Better to keep busy than just sit here."

Emily nodded, glancing at Danny, who was murmuring to himself, sweat coating his face.

"Okay," she said. "Hurry back, Lew."

He smiled at her. "Don't worry." He grabbed the poker and left the room. He checked the front door – locked, then went upstairs to check the windows, which were shut and secure. Back downstairs, he checked the kitchen window then went to check on the back door.

The back door was open, showing the darkness that lurked outside, black as Satan's arsehole, baiting him to come on out. His heartbeat kicked up a notch. Panic gnawed at his guts. He stepped toward the open doorway; the poker quivered just enough to be noticed. The fresh night air hit his lungs; he breathed it in, grateful to be inhaling something other than the stale air inside the house. Danny's blood was drying just outside the door. The night was quiet for the moment, tranquil in its stillness. The kitchen clock ticked away the seconds. He shivered as a dog barked in the distance.

He closed the door, locking it. He was sure he had closed it before, as sure as he had two testicles and a penis. Was something in the house? He stood still, unmoving, listening to the sounds of the house, wood and brick settling together, the breeze skipping around the walls.

Lewis tapped the poker across his palm. There was a weird smell here, like someone had left out some meat in the sun.

Suddenly, Emily screamed.

Lewis ran to the living room, his legs almost giving way when he saw what was waiting for him. He heard himself cry out; his mouth fall open in a moronic expression of fear.

There was something in the house, after all.

Sara was standing before the far wall. In front of her, clinging to the wall like some nightmarish species of octopi, was some kind of tentacled creature, a mass of black flesh and writhing limbs almost as big as the wall itself. The spoiled meat smell was overpowering.

Sara didn't make a sound or show any sign of fear toward the creature.

"Sara!" Emily screamed. "Sara, come back here!"

Danny had awoken from his stupor, and was staring goggle-eyed at the thing on the wall.

Lewis stepped toward his daughter, but she only had eyes for the creature. "Sara, get away from that thing. Sara, please come back here."

In the centre of the creature's mass of tentacles was a fleshy, glistening mass: its main body. A nest of moist, bulbous eyes stared at

Sara.

It was hypnotising her, Lewis realised.

Sara twisted her neck to look at Lewis. She smiled, her face bright and excited as if it were snowing outside.

Emily was crying on the other side of the room.

Sara's eyes drilled into Lewis's. "Don't be scared, Daddy." Then something thin, long and probing whipped out from the creature's main body and pierced the back of her neck; she grimaced as it inched under her skin. She closed her eyes, and when she opened them again, they seemed as if they belonged to someone else; pools of opaque stillness.

"Oh my god, Sara!" Emily was saying. "Help her, Lewis!"

He wanted to reach out to Sara, but he couldn't risk the creature hurting her. He looked at the creature, and he wanted to rip the fucking thing from the wall and throw it outside to the soldiers. Tears stung his eyes. His daughter was being violated by something not meant for this Earth, and he couldn't do a thing about it.

"I will not hurt her," said Sara, turning to him. It was her voice, but it was all wrong. It wasn't her speaking no more than a dummy does when a ventriloquist shoves his hand up its backside.

"I am talking through her," she continued. "She is my vessel for the moment. She is my voice."

His throat had dried up so much Lewis expected to spit out dust when he spoke. "What do you want? Please don't hurt my daughter."

Sara smiled again. Behind her, the nest of eyes regarded Lewis with withering scrutiny.

"I will not hurt her," she said.

Lewis didn't believe the creature, whatever it was. He glanced at Emily, who had backed against the wall; she had knocked over a mug, spilling tea on the carpet, but she hadn't noticed. Her eyes didn't leave Sara. Her throat was moving, like she had swallowed something alive and it was under the skin, scurrying up and down.

"What do you want?" Lewis asked the creature.

"I want to survive," it said through Sara.

"You were in that escape pod," said Danny, sitting up on the sofa.

Sara's eyes flickered toward Danny then back at Lewis. "Yes...your machines destroyed my ship."

"The jets," muttered Lewis.

"You attacked us without warning or cause. We came here to seek shelter…"

"Shelter?" Lewis asked. "You didn't come here to invade us?"

"We have neither the capability or the intent to attack your planet. We are refugees." There was hatred in Sara's voice, sharp as thorns.

"Oh shit," said Danny.

"We came here for help," Sara said. "We were activating the signal lights on our ship, to communicate with you, when your machines attacked us. We were defenceless. All of our ships, all over your world, were attacked."

"I'm sorry," said Lewis. "But it wasn't us personally that attacked you."

Sara said, "If you had done, I would have killed all of you by now."

Lewis shivered; the chill ran down his body, from his head to his toes. He cleared his throat. "What happened to you? Why are you here? Where are you from?"

Sara's eyes turned upward; Lewis knew she wasn't looking at the ceiling. "Not too far away. Our planet was attacked by another species. They overran us; they swarmed our world, destroyed our nests. They wiped out billions of us; a few ships escaped. My family died trying to escape our planet. I had to leave them behind."

Lewis looked past Sara to the creature. "I'm so sorry."

The creature's eyes, all at once, turned to him. Then Sara turned to him, too, her eyes like pockets of dead space. "I came here because I sensed the child; your daughter. She intrigues me. My species does not have children; we emerge from our eggs fully-grown."

"Please let my daughter go," Emily pleaded, from across the room.

Lewis looked at his wife, then back to his daughter. "Please…"

There was a knock on the front door. Lewis swivelled toward the sound, startled. He went to the window, peered from between the curtains. Outside, the soldiers were going from house to house.

The soldiers knocked again, louder. A bead of sweat trickled down Lewis's face. The creature's stink was in his nostrils. He couldn't let the soldiers know the creature was here.

Another series of knocks. Lewis met Emily and Danny's gaze. Sara was staring at him as if she had asked him a question and was awaiting the answer.

"Open up!" a voice ordered. "Open the door or we'll kick it down!"

Lewis sighed through his nose. "Shit." He looked at the creature. "What do we do now?"

Sara's face seemed set in stone. "Answer the door, Lewis. Let them in."

He walked to the door and opened it slowly, leaving a small gap between it and the jamb. The two soldiers, their rifles held with a vague air of menace, regarded him through the dark portals of their gas masks. He held no doubt that they would shoot him given a chance.

"Yes, can I help you?" he said, trying to keep his voice even but failed. The soldiers had noticed.

"Let us in, sir. We're doing a sweep of the area. We need to check each house."

Lewis wasn't sure which one of them said it. "What are you checking for?"

The soldiers didn't answer straight away. Their rifles slowly moved his way. Lewis felt his legs weaken.

"Possible contamination, sir. Now let us in."

"I can't; I have a daughter who's trying to get to sleep."

"Sir," one of the soldiers said. "I recommend that you let us into the house."

Both rifles were now pointed at him; no attempt to disguise it.

Lewis backed away from the door, his heart threatening to burst from his chest. "Okay."

The soldiers were looking at his t-shirt. He followed their gaze. Dried blood stained his t-shirt; it must have got there when he had helped dress Danny's leg wound.

"Inside," one of them said. They barged him out of the doorway and he fell down. The soldiers stormed past him, rifles raised, into the living room.

Lewis rubbed his head, waiting for the gunshots and the screams. He struggled up from the floor. He had to save his family.

He followed the soldiers, and walked into a scene from *The Twilight Zone*.

The soldiers were stood still, their rifles lowered, staring at Sara.

The room fell into dead silence. Lewis hung back in the doorway, unsure of what to do. What were the soldiers doing?

Sara's dark eyes held them in sway, mesmerised.

And then something happened.

The soldiers started to shake, dropping their rifles on the floor. It was if they had both been gripped by seizures. They made small murmuring sounds from underneath their gas masks; these sounds turned to gasps that turned to stifled groans. Lewis felt something in the air, like electricity, tingling on his skin.

The soldiers ripped off their masks, revealing faces not much older than teenagers, and began to claw at their faces. Blood ran from their mouths, ears and noses, running in crimson streams as they stared at Sara. They were choking. Their bodies became quivering wrecks. Their eyes rolled upward into white and their bones cracked with a sound like kindling on a fire.

The soldiers dropped down dead; their last movements were the judder of their limbs as their bodies succumbed to whatever forces had corrupted them.

"Holy shit," Danny said. Lewis agreed with him. Emily could only glance back and forth between the soldiers, Sara and the creature.

Sara looked at them all, ignoring the dead soldiers as if they were discarded scraps of meat. "I had to kill them; they would have killed us all."

Lewis looked at the soldiers. They would be reported missing, eventually.

"Do not feel bad for them," said Sara.

"Please let Sara go," Emily begged the creature again.

Sara smiled, and there was only pity in it. The creature, hanging on the wall like an elaborate Halloween decoration gone wrong, regarded Emily with its many eyes.

"I will release the child," Sara said. "She will not be harmed."

Emily said, "Thank you."

"Thank you," Lewis echoed.

The creature let go of Sara; the probe slipped out from under her skin and returned to its main body. She didn't fall down, which Lewis had expected; she closed her eyes, then snapped them open and she looked at her father. Her eyes had returned to normal; no darkness there, only his daughter's soul.

The creature suddenly shot past Lewis, like a shadow. Its cold flesh touched his skin for an awful millisecond. The reek of spoiled meat flew in his face; he looked at the empty wall then turned to Danny and Emily.

"It went out the front door," said Danny, open-mouthed. "It went out the fucking front door." He let out a hysterical giggle that Lewis could feel building in his own throat.

Emily raced over and hugged Sara, relief and tears in her eyes. They embraced as a family, oblivious of the dead men at their feet.

The soldiers' personal radios stirred with static, then a voice: "Morgan, Corby – come in. Situation report. Any sign of infection? Over."

Lewis looked down at the radios, then at Emily. Danny was leaning over one of the dead soldiers, putting something in his pocket; he fell back onto the sofa, wiping sweat from his face.

"Morgan, Corby…respond. Over."

"What now?" Emily asked. Her hands were gripping Sara's shoulders, a mixture of motherly love and possession. Sara didn't seem to notice; there was a woozy look on her face, as if she just awoke from a dream.

"I don't know," replied Lewis. "We could move the bodies…"

"But they'll know that the soldiers came here," Emily said. "The others will be searching for them."

"She's right," Danny said.

"So what do we do?" Lewis asked. Panic rose inside him. The cloying stink of recent death and blood thickened the air until it felt like he was immersed in liquid. The soldiers' eyes were open, staring at oblivion. Christ, they had been young.

He considered taking the soldiers' weapons, but he didn't have any experience with guns. He'd probably end up shooting himself and his family if he tried to use one of the rifles.

"What's happening?" asked Sara. "What happened to the soldiers?"

"They fell down," said Emily.

Sara touched her mother's arm. "Their names were Robert and David. How do I know that? They won't get up again, will they?"

Emily hesitated. "No, they won't. Not again."

The Lost

Lewis heard a footstep out by the front door. He knew what was coming. He thought he heard the safety of a rifle being taken off. He moved Emily and Sara to the back of the room, near Danny. They all looked at each other, thinking the same thought.

Shadows loomed in the doorway.

Lewis put his arms around his wife and his daughter. Danny glanced at him and winked.

Two soldiers stalked into the room. They saw Lewis and the others, rifles snapping up to sight them. The soldiers halted next to the bodies.

"What the fuck happened here?" one of them asked.

"Looks like the creature got them," the other soldier said, hidden behind the gas mask. "Doesn't matter. We have our orders. Gotta proceed with the purge; can't risk infection."

Lewis kissed Emily and Sara. "I'm sorry," he whispered. Sara was crying. Emily could only look at him, her face tired and scared; but she was beautiful, and he would always remember her as beautiful. His beautiful wife and his beautiful daughter. He nodded once at Danny, who nodded back.

They waited to die.

Then the television burst into life. They all turned toward it, even the soldiers.

The television screen went from darkness to a camera shot of the sky above London. There were lights above the city; hundreds of them.

A nervous voice was talking over the pictures: "...we've lost contact with dozens of cities across the world...There's been unsubstantiated reports of lights appearing over other cities. It appears to be a fleet of UFOs. We're getting information that there are thousands of lights in the sky, all over the world...and they're moving."

The screen turned to static, but there were still snatched pockets of words.

"...lost contact..."

"...thousands of them..."

"...a fleet...city...destroyed..."

"Sounds like bad news," said Danny.

The picture degraded into static and fuzz. The lights flickered.

The soldiers turned away from the television.

Lewis stared at the soldiers, making a point of being defiant to the last, making sure that the soldiers would remember his family's faces for years to come and keep them awake at night.

"Close your eyes," Lewis told his family.

The soldiers tensed, ready to fire.

Lewis braced himself. If he had believed in God, he would have mouthed a silent prayer.

The soldiers suddenly staggered backward. Gunfire filled the room. Their rifles fired, spraying rounds around the room as their bodies spasmodically jerked from the bullets piercing them. Before Lewis shielded his family with his body, he saw Danny firing a pistol at the soldiers.

Emily and Sara were screaming.

Then the gunfire stopped. The room fell silent. Lewis raised his head to look at the room. His ears were ringing, and the air stank of gunpowder.

The soldiers were dead, slumped against the wall under the window.

"Danny," he said, "what…"

Lewis turned to his friend, and Danny was staring back at him; but Danny couldn't see him…Danny couldn't see anything. Danny's face only had one side left. A bullet had ripped away the other side. The wall around him, and the sofa, was littered with bullet holes.

Danny must have stolen the pistol from one of the dead soldiers.

Lewis sat in numbed silence. Eventually, Emily and Sara looked up, looking around the room with the same dumb shock that throbbed inside him.

They embraced in this room of killing, which had once been their home. And Lewis knew then that they couldn't stay here.

"We have to leave," he said.

* * *

Lewis took a pistol from one of the soldiers. He would use it if he had to. Emily and Sara gathered some food, their personal documents and some supplies, and put them in a rucksack.

Then they said goodbye to Danny and covered him with a

blanket.

The other soldiers would be here soon, Lewis knew. They had to leave the village; the village was being gradually wiped out. There was gunfire and screams in the distance. Too many screams. Hell had found the village and made its home here.

They left the house through the back door, hoping to keep to the darkness and reach the woods behind the house. Emily told Sara that they were going on holiday, on a camping trip, but the girl was still sobbing silently, held in Lewis's arms.

As they crossed the field that led to the woods, a great light flared on the horizon, southward. The night turned to twilight.

"Is that Basingstoke?" asked Emily.

"Not anymore," replied Lewis. Another light bloomed in the east. "And that was Reading, I think."

They kept going; there was nothing else to do. Lewis heard shouts and raised voices behind them. He saw the searching beams of torches raking the field. In the strange light of the explosion, he saw the soldiers hunting them; fast, stalking figures in the half-gloom.

"Stop!" a voice commanded. More torchlight coming from the edge of the field. "Stop or we fire!"

"Keep running!" Lewis shouted. "Don't look back!"

They ran; Lewis made sure he stayed behind Emily and Sara. His legs were hurting already. Ahead, the woods loomed, promising sanctuary. Lewis kicked his legs, ignoring the extra weight of carrying Sara.

The torchlight found them; Lewis stumbled, almost dropping her.

Shots rang out, echoing across the field. Sara screamed.

Emily was suddenly thrown off her feet, bullets ripping into her; she was dead before she hit the floor. Lewis and Sara screamed. Tracer rounds whizzed past their heads and kicked up dirt around their feet. Lewis tripped and fell down next to his wife. He spilled Sara onto the ground. Sara was reaching for Emily, calling for her mother, her voice shrill. The air was alive with the hot rain of bullets. The torchlight was getting closer. The circle was closing.

Lewis grabbed Sara, shielding her. "You have to run for the woods, Sara!"

"I don't want to go," she said, tears rolling down her face. "I don't want to leave you and Mummy!"

He tried to smile for her; it was all he could do not to break down in front of her. "It's OK, darling. Me and Mummy will be right behind you, don't worry. Mummy's just injured. I need to take care of her."

"Daddy…"

"You have to run, Sara. Don't be afraid. We'll see you again soon." He handed her the rucksack.

She stared into his eyes, as if searching for the lie. Tears streaked down her face. Then, without a word, she kissed him on the cheek, hugged him and ran away.

"Don't look back, Sara," Lewis whispered. He watched her vanish into the darkness around the woods. Then he took the pistol from his pocket. He looked down at Emily; he would be with her soon. He turned toward the soldiers.

"Bastards," he muttered. He thought of Danny, and he thought of Emily, and he thought of Sara. He only hoped she would make it out of the village.

Lewis stood up, raised the pistol and emptied the magazine at the approaching figures. The gun clicked empty, but he still kept pressing the trigger until a great force pushed him to the ground; there was a terrible heat in his chest and stomach. A blazing pain. He looked down at the bleeding holes the bullets had made. He exhaled one of his final breaths and turned his head to look at Emily. Her eyes were open as if she was looking at him, welcoming him into death. Was there a smile on her face?

Lewis reached out and closed his hand around hers. The pain wasn't so bad now. His mind began slipping away.

The soldiers stood over him, faces hidden by masks.

"Hurry up," Lewis said to them. "Get it over with."

They did.

* * *

Sara ran through the woods, not looking back. The darkness seemed to close in around her, silently calling her name. The soldiers – the bad men – were in the field. They were shouting. They had made her Mummy and Daddy dead. She knew Mummy and Daddy were gone, and the sadness was like a blooming flower in her chest; a terrible, poisonous flower.

So she did what her Daddy had told her to do: she ran with all the speed her legs gave her, deeper into the woods where the soldiers couldn't find her. Dead leaves crunched under her feet. She ran for what seemed like hours, never looking back, never looking behind her. When she stopped running, she leaned against a tree, getting her breath back. There were more sounds of distant gunfire. She didn't want to think about what the soldiers were doing to the rest of the people in the village. What had they done to all of her friends? Were all of her friends like Mummy and Daddy now?

Tears poured down her face. She raised her face to the canopy and saw the night sky past the twisted, reaching tree branches.

Something was moving in the darkness nearby, grabbing her attention.

Sara pressed her back against the tree, keeping silent. The rustle of leaves and the creak of branches. Something was moving toward her. She waited. She wasn't afraid anymore.

A shadow, darker than the dark, appeared before her, hanging from a tree branch as if it had been waiting for her. It was the creature, and it spoke to her within her mind, its voice calm like her mother's used to be when she tucked Sara into bed.

HELLO, SARA. DON'T BE SCARED.

"I'm not," she said. It was true; despite the creature's ugliness, she felt no fear toward it, only sympathy.

GOOD. YOU SHOULDN'T BE SCARED OF ME. I'M SORRY ABOUT YOUR PARENTS.

"What do you want?"

I'VE COME TO SAVE YOU. I'VE BEEN WAITING FOR YOU. WE ARE LINKED NOW. WE ARE DIFFERENT BUT THE SAME.

Sara could only stare at the creature.

YOU SHOULD COME WITH ME NOW, SARA. THIS WORLD WILL BE CONQUERED BY THE SAME SPECIES THAT CONQUERED MINE. THEY WILL DRAIN THIS WORLD. THEY HAVE ALREADY DESTROYED SOME OF YOUR CITIES…THEY WILL DESTROY THE REST IN TIME. THEY WILL DESTROY YOUR ARMIES. THEY WILL ENSLAVE YOUR RACE. BUT IF YOU COME WITH ME, I WILL PROTECT YOU AND YOU WILL BE SAFE AND YOU WILL SURVIVE.

The soldiers were hunting her, and they wouldn't give up. The creature was right. She felt a connection with it, a part of it within her, melding with her. They were different, but the same. And she didn't want to be alone. She needed someone to take care of her.

"Okay," Sara said. There were explosions far away. Past the trees, flames filled the horizon. The village, her home, was gone.

GOOD, SARA. GOOD. I WILL LOOK AFTER YOU FROM NOW ON, AND YOU WILL LOOK AFTER ME.

And with the world burning and the woods as deep and black as a fairy tale forest, she went off into the darkness with her new companion.

CHEMPLANTIUM
BY DANE T. HATCHELL

Greetings, my name is Enadious B. Neuman. I am sending this transmission through the great voids of space in hopes of making contact with other civilizations in this vast universe.

This document is part of my memoirs, just one of many chapters. I hope to give you a sense of what it was like as I spent my life working on Chemplantium, one of my Homeworld's artificial metal moons, of which is one of two. The other is Refinerium. Refinerium's purpose is to refine zoil for the planet's energy usage. Chemplantium uses waste streams and special cuts of zoil for chemicals production. It should be obvious to the reader why hazardous processes such as these inspired the nations on Homeworld to build the metal moons and move production from the surface of our planet.

Chemplantium has been in operation for over one-hundred years. I worked there for nearly forty. It was a wonderful place, where the many races of our world learned to overcome physical and cultural differences.

My name is Enadious, and this a chapter from my life.

* * *

There was excitement in the air. No, I'm not talking about some pheromone that 'Cord was secreting out of one of his anal holes. The Comet Chronos had entered the solar system and was hurtling toward the sun. Every thirty years, the mighty giant would make its rendezvous and then head back into the dark of space.

Chronos is a fast moving comet. From the time that it passes Homeworld, rounds the sun, and makes its pass by again, it takes only 12 hours. As a tradition, it is during those twelve hours that children of our home world make wishes in hopes that the Creator will make them come true. It's all in fun, and with a little help from parents, a lot of the children's wishes do come true. Perhaps you have similar traditions on your world.

Me, D'uane, 'Cord, Barbix, Dekulos, and Loft-Yard were on the D shift waiting to view the Comet from the forward window of Oxo sector. A fresh pot of jabba had finished dripping and everyone was enjoying cup, I like mine black.

"This one time, at Dweble camp, I stuck a balerry up my..."

"Barbix," I yelled. "How many times do we have to tell you that some things are better kept to yourself?"

Barbix was a good kid. Couldn't handle his jabba though. His race was known for being high-strung. He was an average sized Dweble, about 200 pounds of protoplasm that could take any form. Dwebles were a curious sort; evolution never gave them the need to mate. When mature enough, Dwebles shed about five pounds of protoplasm that eventually develop a sense of consciousness. A creature possible of a thousand faces, and a billion observations. Man, they sure had a way of getting on your nerves. One redeeming factor, the ability of Barbix to take the form of a well-proportioned female had a way of making time pass on the late shift.

D'uane slowly lifted his right arm and grabbed the bill of his cap. He slowly lifted it, scratched his head and muttered, "Ha...that was some predicament we sure got into."

D'uane's race shared some common ancestors as 'Cord's, but they were different in many ways. D'uane's race, the SBD, consumed only one thing: B'udlyte. B'udlyte is toxic to every other race on Homeworld. But his kind has evolved to process this toxin, thus ensuring an abundant food supply over the ages. One other thing, the toxic food also produces toxic gas. Thus, for any member of that race to intermingle with all other races, a filter made into underwear must be worn at all times. No, it doesn't filter odor, and to the Creator I wish it would, just the toxins. There is no sound made when gas is passed to give you a heads up to find a way out.

Before D'uane could continue the story, it finally appeared. The Comet Chronos! It was beautiful. It glowed dominantly emerald, with traces of blue, red, and yellow swirling inside. A breathtaking sight as viewed from space without the atmosphere to filter out any of its glory. We gathered around the forward window and marveled.

'Chord broke wind in sequence through his four anal openings, to the tune of his tribe's anthem. 'Chord's race could eat any organic matter and process it through one of its four stomachs. He usually stored up enough gas to fart a tune up to sixteen notes. He was quite talented; still, you did have to use your imagination.

Chemplantium

* * *

Much sooner than we would have liked, Chronos slipped out of view; it would be several hours before it would return to say goodbye.

Nights grow long and lonely on Chemplantiem, even though you are never really alone. Usually at the beginning of the shift, everyone is cutting up and telling jokes. As the night drags on, everyone drifts into his or her own individual space.

As I looked out of the south window of the control room, I was surprised to see Volteer. His hair was standing straight up as usual, his collar crooked. He stared through the outside window where we were standing earlier, as if waiting for Chronos. He held his jabba cup firmly in hand, and would lift to his lips occasionally.

I gave him a small wave, but got no response. It was a little odd that an AE would be at his post at this time of the night. As a race, Afterbirth Entities found their place in society in the computer programming trade. Which generally took place on the day shift.

Getting up from the plush Controller chair, I stretched, wandered out of the control room and took a spot by Volteer's side.

"Volteer...Volteer?"

"Uh, oh, Yes Enadious?"

"Looks like you're up late tonight. Is there a problem with the Xperion system?"

"No, nothing work involved."

"Your wife kicked you out of the Engineering Complex?"

"No."

"Volteer, help me out here. What do you want?"

"I have this feeling. That things are about to get much worse for all of us." With that, Volteer turned away and walked to his office without even looking back. My eyes followed him until he was out of sight.

Being away from my control station wasn't wise. The thought of a cup of jabba before I returned to my post sounded good, and I made my way toward the pot.

Back in my chair, the jabba cup had almost reached my lips when the hotline rang. This was never a good thing. Fearing the worse, I picked up the phone.

"Enadious, this is Fank," he spoke before I had a chance to say hello.

"Fank, aren't you on patrol?" Fank was my brother, in Near Space Security, and called me from time to time. Never on the hotline though.

"Not now, I'm on the station. Listen, there are terrorists from Quari on Chemplantiem. We are not sure of their location, our info is not complete."

"Fank, security has never been better around here. Maybe your info is wrong." I had two ID badges and at least two card readers to pass before I was allowed to enter any areas that required protecting.

"No, the information is correct. We have found two breach pods on the outside skin. They are here and inside. Alert everyone on the Oxo sector, mode yellow, repeat: mode yellow. Meet me at B5 in 5 minutes. Out!"

I pushed the alert switch and made the all-call for everyone to secure their work areas. The unit controls were set to safe mode to minimize damage in case of an attack.

The sector warden checked everyone off his list as each arrived back into the Control Center. I noticed as I left to meet Fank, the snack synthesizer man was here to fill the machine with *spoo*. Well, at least we won't go hungry during the lockdown.

It occurred to me that Volteer didn't show up for the head count. So, I made a slight detour to the AE's office.

"Volteer...look, there has been a.."

The next thing I knew I was face down on the floor. My head was pounding from the concussion of the blast. Slowly I came too, not sure of where I was or what had happened. My thoughts were, *I'm at work...I'm on the floor...I don't remember this being a performance review...oh yeah,...Fank...Terrorists! My Creator! Terrorists!*

Volteer helped me up to a sitting position. "Terrorists! What do we do?" I shouted. "I was on my way to meet with Fank, but the explosion... the control room!"

Volteer grabbed my arm and helped me up and down the hallway, raw fear gnawing a hole in my stomach.

The sight was almost indescribable. D'uane, 'Cord, Barbix, Deku-los, and Loft-Yard were dead, burned to a crisp. How could this be? Then it hit me, the *spoo* man. He must have been the terrorist. He was a walking bomb. I wondered what caused a burn in the floor that opened a hole to the next level down?

"You said you were going to meet this Fank fellow, we can't help here. Let's go Enadious, let's go now!" Volteer pulled me away and we ran toward B5.

* * *

Fank was waiting as we rounded the corner. "Enadious! Are you all right?"

"No, No I'm not all right! They're dead! They're all dead!"

"Get hold of yourself, man! How many terrorists did you count?"

"One...only one," I managed to say as I choked up.

"These terrorists always travel in pairs. The other can't be far behind! Did you get any reports from the Nova Sector?"

"No." Then I realized where I was standing. "This hall leads to the flux reactors!"

Fank shot me a look of confidence. "My men are in position to protect it. Come on, we'll meet up with them." The sound of our footsteps echoed down the hall as we ran to meet with a hoard of troops guarding the flux reactor entrance.

"Status!" Fank demanded as he approached the commander.

"Two explosions with 15 dead, Oxo sector and Nova sector."

"Why? Why damnit? What can they hope to gain by killing a few people?" Fank was sorting the situation aloud.

"Wait...General Fank...I 'm getting an update communication," said the commander, adjusting the radio piece in his ear. "General, sir, the explosions were a diversion. We have the remaining six terrorists holed up in A12."

"Well, let's go smoke them out," Fank said with a far away glean in his eyes.

"It is not that simple, general," the commander continued, "the terrorists are Bio-bombs."

"Bio-bombs, what is he talking about, Fank?" I asked.

"Years ago," he explained, "a compound, *plantoone,* was created that acted on calcium in the body. Various levels of this compound can bring about different results. One such mixture, when ingested, causes the calcium in the skeletal system to super heat. This causes the water in the body to expand and start to break down to the basic elements hydrogen and oxygen. The process happens so rapidly that the body explodes and the heat and blast kill people near the explosion. The skeleton itself becomes so hot it will burn through anything underneath it as it melts."

"Yes, that makes sense. I saw the burned bodies. I saw the hole in the floor."

Fank pointed upward. "Well, it is time for revenge now. We'll blast them through the walls and not give them a chance to get us. Forward, we move!"

"No, general, we can't," cautioned the commander. "The terrorists have positioned themselves on A12. That means they are located just above the flux reactors. If we try to take them out, they'll swallow a plantoone pellet and burn through the floor straight into the flux reactors. Chemplantiem would not survive such an attack."

Fank wondered aloud again, "What are they really up to? If they want to destroy Chemplantium they would do so right now."

"General, we have the terrorist's demands; they want a universal access module and the codes to the Jaebird, your patrol ship. If you refuse, the flux reactors will be destroyed. They give us 10 minutes to comply."

"My ship? Why my ship? These terrorists are not concerned about their lives. They wouldn't leave an opportunity to destroy everything here unless they could trade it for something that would cause even more destruction." Fank's face flushed red as he realized the true plan. These terrorists could take his ship and overload its flux reactor, then send it down toward Homeworld and explode it over a major city. Millions and millions were at risk. What little time was left, was quickly ticking away.

A view monitor on the wall showed the Comet Chronos, returning from around the sun and on its way back into space. I looked at it and thought about all the wishes I had made as a child.

Volteer's consciousness invaded my thoughts. "Enadious...**WHO** are you?"

"What? We don't have time for you AE mind games. I'm a man who will never see one *dribble* of retirement pay. Pardon me now while I bend over and kiss my ass goodbye!"

"No Enadious, it is time for you to act." Volteer pointed toward the flux reactors.

"H..How, Volteer, how?"

"The future is always purchased in the past. You must go back and ensure the future."

"No more riddles Volteer! How?" He was starting to piss me off.

Volteer removed his eyeglasses, and handed them to me. "Take it; it is not what it appears to be. The glasses are made of exotic matter, and are valued at more than you could make in 100 lifetimes. It will allow you passage back in time. Hold the glasses tightly and run toward the flux reactors. The exotic matter in the glasses will catch the waves of the flux field and you will be able to ride the waves to a previous time."

Volteer made a hand gesture and door one to the flux reactors opened; a warm hum filled the air.

"Now see here," Fank said, "on whose authority are you doing this?"

"Yours," Volteer added, "and you shall go with him." Volteer made another gesture with his hand and the second door to the flux reactor opened. The exotic matter in my hand started to warm. Then it gently pulled me toward the reactors.

"Come Fank, the past calls us!" I screamed.

"You leave the present at the return of Chronos. You will arrive thirty years in the past at the Coming of Chronos. You must return to the flux reactor as Chronos rounds the sun and makes its leave approaching Chemplantium; you will arrive back here in our time at the coming of Chronos. It will be up to you to prevent all that has happened. Be careful of your actions, you will have to live with them in your future." Volteer watched the two run forward, and then, wink out of time in a bright white light.

* * *

Fank and I ran as fast as we could, but the air started getting so thick that I felt like I was plowing through thick mud. We were slowing, time was slowing, to the point that everything suddenly... stopped! Fank and I felt so light I thought we might float. Then time returned to normal.

"Whew. Fank, what happened?" I started feeling normal again. "Are we there yet?"

"You mean, are we *when* yet?"

We looked around, things did look different. Newer and cleaner, the surroundings looking primitive and bulkier. We got a surprise when we looked at each other.

"Fank, we're naked!"

Fank adjusted his genitals. "Those flux waves warmed me up so much I didn't realize it. We've got to find some clothes soon or we won't last here long."

My eyes went to my hand that held the glasses, and I breathed a sigh of relief. "I still have the glasses. Thank the creator. I wonder why we lost everything else during the time jump?"

"Not sure, guess because it's made of exotic matter. Strange stuff, applications are highly classified."

I was relieved that no one else was around. The glasses started to warm again in my hand and I realized that we had to get out now. Pointing to the left, I motioned Fank to a hallway; I knew where a supply room was.

"Enadious, do you think we're in the time period we think we are?"

"Things look a lot like I remember from 27 years ago. I'm glad we arrived before I was hired on. I don't know what would happen if I met myself in the past."

Fank didn't respond, he knew time travel was very dangerous. I had heard theories of what would happen if a person met himself earlier in time. Some scenarios were quite devastating.

We came to a supply room door, luck was with us. A good amount of clothing, work boots, and other necessities a maintenance worker would need were arranged neatly on shelves. As we dressed, I felt my dignity return.

"With these disguises, we could practically hide in plain sight," I said. "No one pays attention to maintenance workers." I stopped cold. "What do we do, Fank? What can we do now that in 30 years it'll make a difference?"

"That is the 10,000 *dribble* question. We need a plan, the comet Chronos should be appearing now so we have only hours to figure this out. The sad reality is that the terrorists arrived in the breach pods before the sighting of the Comet. When we return, we will have to find them and kill them before they can make it to Oxo and Nova, and take control of A12. We'll need weapons."

"Why not just when we get back, warn the others before the terrorists make a move?"

"The terrorists will already be there. We don't have time to convince anyone of our story. We are going to have to take them out before they get into position. Also, we must make sure that we don't make contact with ourselves when we return to Chemplantiem. It is possible that if we meet ourselves in the future, it could cause all time and space to rip apart."

"Oh, is that all?"

"Yeah, I've been thinking about it a lot. I don't know what's going to happen when we get back. Will there be two of us? I don't know, and we can't worry about it. We must acquire weapons and take out the terrorists as quickly as possible and try not to be detected when we get back." Fank rubbed his stubbly chin. "Where can we get weapons? Security on this metal moon is allowed nothing stronger than a pain stick. We need something that slings metal from a distance; we have to surprise and kill the terrorists."

I thought a moment. "I believe I know how we can get a couple of blasters. It all depends if a certain person is on shift." Fate had given us a chance, and I was depending on destiny for this thing to work out. Known to only his workmates, one of the Oxo sectors Controllers carried a blaster in each of his boots. He was stable enough that no one feared for their immediate safety, but unstable enough that if someone reported it and got him fired, well, no one was willing to take that chance. P'lee, was his name, and debauchery was his game.

Fank and I slowly shuffled down the hallways leading to the Oxo sector. Along the way, we found another supply room and grabbed a couple of water buckets and mops. This gave us perfect cover as we mopped our way into the control room, keeping our heads low, and not making any eye contact with the others.

I recognized the man on the control board immediately, it was C'uz! My how young and thin he looked. It brought back a flood of memories, of times we worked together before he retired. He had his, or someone else's blade and was in the process of putting a sharp edge on it. Open on the Controller's desk was a copy of a porn magazine with two women spread naked on C'uz's tribe's flag. Ah, the good old days.

I looked around and didn't see P'lee anywhere. This didn't leave me with a good feeling. I didn't know if he was on vacation or off shift or in jail. The clock was still ticking.

Fank made his way to an office where the lights were off; he went in to look for information. A manning board on the wall showed P'lee was indeed on shift today. Listed by his name was a note for him to be at Medlab at 0200. Looking at a timepiece on the wall, in just a half an hour. Fank quietly headed for the door.

"Enadious!" whispered Fank, "Come here." I mopped my way over to Fank. "P'lee is on his way to Medlab. We need to go now." We wasted no time leaving the Oxo sector, Medlab wasn't that far away.

P'lee was handing the paperwork to a nurse behind a desk as we arrived. His mouth was wide with an evil smile and he licked his eyebrows with his forked tongue. She ignored him. He had jet-black hair greased down on his head, combed over to the right. His skin was starting to peal under his jaw, he would be molting soon. He was a card-carrying member of the race of Pr'vrts, but you wouldn't have to see his card to figure that out.

P'lee sat in a waiting area reading a magazine; we had to figure out a way to get into the office and past the receptionist.

Fank motioned to me to go down the hall. "There has got to be a back way in," reasoned Fank. "Look over there, a couple of laundry carts." Sure enough, at the back of Medlab there were two swinging doors with two large laundry carts. The carts were filled with Medical clothing set for cleaning. We changed quickly.

Neither of us had an ID Badge, and no one could work in Medlab without an ID. So, we loaded our arms in clothing from the laundry cart, blocking any view of where our badge should be. We entered the building without causing any attention and begun our search.

I stopped and listened at each door down the east wing, Frank did the same on the west. Finally, I heard a distinct voice telling a joke. My mind was flooded with memories of the few years that I had worked with P'lee, my bowels quivered a little.

"What do you tell an adopted *Dweble* when it wants to go out and play? Shut up and keep on sucking!" the voice roared with laughter.

Yes, it was P'lee all right. The doctor didn't respond. I still shudder when I think about P'lee. Wondering what to do next, the decision was made when the door opened and the doctor and P'lee made an exit passed me.

"Go see the nurse at the end of the hall and get your vitals checked. When finished, come see me in the Image Room so I can take an inside look at your kidneys." The doctor said.

P'lee left the room without wearing his boots. His boots were exactly where he kept his blasters. When the halls became clear, I opened the room door, and slipped inside.

Set on the side on the wall with P'lee's over shirt covering them sat the two boots. My heart skipped a beat as I moved the shirt, and YES! A blaster in each boot! I thought briefly about kissing them, but the odor from the boots discouraged that sign of appreciation. Hiding the blasters on the inside of my waistband, I left out of the room and down the hall and met up with Fank.

"I've got 'em Fank, two of them! What's the plan now? Time is almost up. How can we bring these back?"

"We can't bring them back, you know that. So, they need to be in a certain place when we return to the future. A certain place that won't be bothered for 30 years until we retrieve them.

I then came up with an idea.

Arriving back at Oxo, Fank and I headed straight for the Oxo trophy display cabinet. The clear-plaz doors held memorabilia from events in Oxo's past. Some images of employee's were there, and two trophies from the old Oxo tuball team. The cap easily popped off each of the hollow tuballs and a blaster fit snugly in the space. After snapping the tuball back together, I gently closed the door, and wiped the smudge away from the handle. We both breathed a sigh of relief, only to be startled from a voice behind us.

"Hey, you two, get over here and give me a hand!" It was C'vetta, an Oxo supervisor. Fank and I looked at each other thinking we were busted. But that was not the case.

"Hey, come on now or you'll be looking for work somewhere else tomorrow!"

We walked toward C'vetta, who turned and led us to a side office.

"We need to get these boxes over to transport now, don't want to miss the shuttle."

I was familiar with transport, and this was not the protocol. Whatever C'vetta was doing, it was not legal. Fank and I loaded the boxes on the transcarts and followed C'vetta to the shipping docks. There was no one there to inspect the packages; this certainly was not an approved shipment.

Whatever was in the boxes, I had a feeling it would bring in a lot of dribbles on the black market. This surely wasn't the first time C'vetta did this, and certainly wouldn't be the last. The ship was loaded and made its way out of the docks and then into space.

I looked to C'vetta and said, "We need to go now. Our foreman will be looking for us."

C'vetta's eyes narrowed as he pulled out a pain stick from behind some pallets. "I don't think so. I just caught you two loading thousands of *dribbles* worth of stolen supplies. I am going to call security and collect a reward for your capture. If you resist", he tapped the pain stick on the ground with a shower of sparks as evidence that it was powered up.

"Fank we're running out of time. The Comet is about to leave. We have to get to the flux reactors or be trapped here for 30 years," I warned.

"Stop talking," C'vetta said. "One more word and you both go down. I'm contacting security now. What a shame I couldn't stop the shuttle," he said with a broad smile.

Fank pointed his left index finger at C'vetta. The tip pivoted back, shooting a projectile with a soft pop. C'vetta was knocked back, but didn't fall over. Standing there, he slowly started to wobble. Vapor emitted from his body, then it melted into itself, leaving a small pile of meat sizzling on the ground, until it disappeared.

"Fank! What did you do?"

"My finger is an artificial replacement. It is also capable of firing a pellet of a mixture of *plantoone* that is supposed to convert the calcium in the body slow enough so as not to explode as in the terrorists, but enough to totally melt the body. Bones, skin, and all."

Fank took command. "We don't have much time. Come! We must head to the flux reactor room. The Comet is passing!"

Down the halls, we ran. Our minds racing in anticipation for the next mission. That one held the power of life and death. It would take everything we had to pull it off.

Fank started to slow his pace. I looked back and saw him sweating profusely. "Fank? Fank you all right?"

"Enadious...I...I..think the *plantoone* pellets in my finger may be...leaking." Those were the last words Fank spoke. His body started smoking, in no time the vapor disappeared and nothing was left. I can't put into words how I felt at that moment, it happened so quickly.

I broke out of my despair and headed for the flux reactors.

Raising my hand with the glasses toward the first flux reactor door, it opened and then door two also. The glasses started to heat and a hum filled the air. I was on my way back to the future.

* * *

It was the return of the Comet Chronos. Everyone was gathered in the control room to view the comet in the forward window. All were marveling at this wonderful sight. I was later told that at first no one even noticed when I suddenly vanished.

I made it back to my time, the reactors were as I remembered them when I left. The eyeglasses of exotic matter, gone. Clothing, gone. And I remembered Fank, gone too.

Stumbling toward the reactor door, a large yellow fire blanket provided cover for my manhood. I exited the flux reactor room and headed straight for the Oxo sector.

The few people I ran past in the hall, gave me some strange looks. It didn't matter, I was a man driven.

There were no security alarms going off. That was a good sign that the terrorists had not made their move yet.

The sign above read "Oxo Sector" and I turned the corner and headed straight for the trophy case. Inside sat the tuball trophies covered with a fine layer of dust. The tops popped off easily and I was in the possession of two of the finest blasters that history could provide.

The terrorists who blew up Oxo and Nova had been disguised as snack synthesizer vendors. Avoiding main halls in the Oxo sector, I headed for B17.

After nearly 27 years on the job, I knew my way around a bit. There was a certain maintenance panel that I could use to hide in and wait to ambush the terrorists as they made their way to the Oxo sector.

After securing my position, I peered out of a vent hole to see the two snack vendors as they entered the hall. One of the terrorists was heading to Oxo, the other Nova. Both wore the same disguise. Hey, everyone loves the snack man and would never suspect them.

Taking the blaster off safety, I slowly opened the panel. My finger squeezed the trigger and fired two shots quickly. As the bodies hit the floor, the job became complete as I ran up to them and put a slug in each head.

My whole being was numb. Numb from fear, and numb from rage. The problem now was the other six terrorists. Fank never had a chance to formulate a plan on how to handle that bunch. They needed to be ambushed too. More lives would be lost if there were a show-down at A12. Where were they?

"Enadious! Where in the heck have you been? Look at you! Did you slip in the shower? Hey, what are you doing with those blasters?" It was Dekulos. He noticed the two bodies on the floor, just as the alarm sounded mode Yellow.

"Dekulos. These are terrorists. There are six more on Chemplan-tium and we have to find them before they reach A12. Tell me, why did you ask where I have been? Tell me, it's important."

"Well, we were watching Chronos when, for lack of a better way to say, you disappeared."

One of my fears was now gone, I had hoped beyond hope that this is what would happen when I returned to the future. It wasn't possi-ble for me to exist as two in one time period. When I appeared back at the flux reactor, I replaced myself in the Control Center. The Universe had a way to keep order. That meant that Fank was here too. Fank was alive. Because we had not left to return to the past yet. And if we could handle things right this time, there would be no need to. With-out a further word, I took off in a full run toward A12.

Fank was in an office, waiting for communications about the ter-rorists. A call came in and he answered, "Yes."

"General Fank, we have some one here that claims to be your brother," said the commander.

"Well, check his ID and send him up if it's him."

"It's not quite that easy, he has no ID. He has no clothing. He says he has information on the terrorists."

Fank left the office in a slow trot. He arrived to see me naked save for the blanket wrapped over my private parts.

"Enadious! Have you been drinking? What..."

"Fank. They're going to A12. They're loaded with *plantoone*. They…"

"General Fank", the commander interrupted, "we just received word that the terrorists have taken over A12 and have demands that if we don't meet will result in the destruction of Chemplantium."

"Enadious, how did you know?"

I told the story of our adventure in the past. Even the part where he died from the leaking *plantoone* pellet. Fank had a look of disbelief on his face. But he knew it had to be true. I had known about his artificial finger and everything.

We now had a few minutes to defeat the terrorists, or all was lost. I had a plan, and made a call to the Oxo sector. After the call I told Fank, "You must give in to the terrorist's demands."

* * *

The terrorists were pleased, but skeptical. They wanted the universal access module and the codes to the Jaebird. They wanted it in their hands now so they could maneuver the Jaebird in their line of sight from A12's window. Only that way, they would agree to leave the ship, and spare Chemplantium. This would give them the ability to overload the Jaebird's flux reactor and send it to Homeworld. Without the need to leave Chemplantium.

There was another specific demand: the person delivering the access module must be completely naked. Terrorists are not the trusting sort.

The module was carefully loaded in a soft bag. D'uane picked it up and gradually carried it to a main door on A12. The terrorists viewed him from the inside cam. Satisfied that everything was in order, the door opened. D'uane walked in cautiously.

"On the table, do not try to trick us," the burly alien from the planet Quari said.

D'uane complied, gently laying the bag on the table, and backed away slowly.

The lead terrorist's face broke out in a great grin. "We have won! We have defeated the enemy. Nothing can stop us now. There will be songs of the great death that we bring to their Homeworld! *Gwanda* be praised, *Gwanda* be praised!" All the terrorists lifted their fist in the air. *"Gwanda* be praised, *Gwa...,"* And with that all the terrorists fell to the ground with a series of thumps. None were moving or breathing, showing no signs of life at all.

D'uane scratched the back of his head and broke a wicked little smile. He did well, he saved Chemplantium. When you are a member of the tribe of SBD, you are capable of being silent but deadly. The terrorist played right into my plan. D'uane was able to break wind without the interference of his underwear filter, and was able to pass his toxic gas to the demise of the terrorists.

* * *

Needles to say, I sat down on the first chair I could find after A12 was secure. The flood of emotions, physical exhaustion, the Creator only knows what time travel and those flux waves did to my body. History had been changed where not one member of the metal moon was killed or even injured. I sat in silence, giving thanks that it was over.

"Fine work Enadious, even though your story is still difficult to believe," Fank said.

"It is hard for me to believe it myself. Well, it's over now and to-morrow is another shift." I found my legs and got up to go and find a shower. "Oh, look, management is here to thank me."

J'kins, a day superintendant, arrived unexpectedly with two members of security. "Enadious, you know it is illegal to own or oper-ate blasters anywhere on Chemplantium, violating Code 7693."

I protested, "I saved Oxo, I saved Nova, I saved millions of lives on Homeworld!"

"Yes, and I personally thank you. But laws are laws and you are guilty of breaking a very serious one. You did the right thing Enadi-ous; you just went about it the wrong way. You will be taken to a cell, and appear before a judge and a jury of your peers. May the Creator be with you."

With that, J'kins left as I was carried away by the two guards, my heels dragged on the floor.

* * *

It is said on my world that everyone will have his day in court. I never thought mine would come this way. I was familiar with the laws and the justice system on Chemplantium. Justice was swifter and cruder than on Homeworld. At least I was able to represent myself.

The prosecution was represented by J'kins. The judge was Es'mon. The jury of my peers included G'wayne, Bo'kins, and Loft-Yard. Even though Loft-Yard had two heads, they shared one body, thus allowed one vote.

The courtroom was set. Everyone was in place. J'kins started and for his one time period allotment presented the Chemplantium posted offenses according to the written rules. In my time period, I presented all the details of why my actions were honorable and why I should be pardoned. As my time came to the end, Es'mon smashed his fist on his desk and pointed to the jury.

"The trial is over. Each side of the truth have been spoken. Leave now, but return when the vote is ready."

"We hear and comply with our duty," the members of the jury said in unison, and exited the courtroom.

At least the wait was brief. I was hopeful, but concerned. I knew J'kins was only doing his job, he did present a sound case. Nothing untrue was said about me. That was the reason I was so concerned of the final vote.

Judge Es'mon pounded the desk with his fist, breaking the lull in the courtroom. "It is done. The jury is ready to vote. Bring them forth."

The jury positioned themselves to the side of the room, facing both the judge and the rest in the courtroom. Standing, each wearing a full robe black in color, gently tied at the waist.

"Juror one, what of you?" asked Es'mon.

G'waye parted his robe and revealed his sex organ.

Thank goodness, I thought. That was one vote in my favor.

"Juror two, what of you?" continued Es'mon.

Bo'kins parted his robe in the front and voted with me also.

That was two in my favor. But I needed all three or I would have to be tried again.

Es'mon frowned. "Juror Two, could you pick that thing off the floor? You don't want to leave a wet spot. Juror three, what of you?"

The silence of the room was deafening. I always wanted to use that line, but for me, it was actually true. Time seemed frozen. Loft-Yard parted his robe and...Yes! Another vote with me! It was over. I had never been so happy to see another man's sex organ in my life.

And what a sex organ it was. Due to the industrial accident where G'yard and Loft'us were fused together into one person, their sex organ looked like a chocolate vanilla swirl. G'yard was from a black skinned tribe and Lof'tus a white.

I was free, absolved of any wrongdoing.

* * *

A new day, a new shift, the nightmare of the trial behind me. I settled back in my chair at the Controller station, Enadious in control at the Oxo Sector once again. Just like old times, only better.

Barbix entered the control room, skipping on three legs. He stopped and moved his head up to mine. His eyes bulged like a telescope toward me. His mouth contorted from his upper jaw to his lower jaw. "Enadious! What are you doing here?"

"I'm working, just like you. This is D shift you know."

"No! You're not supposed to be here. You're supposed to be in jail."

"No, in case you haven't heard, I had my trial and I won. I was pardoned and allowed to come back to work."

"No!" Barbix protested. "I heard about the trial and I heard that you had a hung jury. I know my Chemplantium rules. The book says that if the jury doesn't all vote the same the defendant has to wait in the cell until the next trial session. I heard you had a hung jury so you should be back in your cell!"

"Barbix...Barbix....Barbix." I sighed and shook my head. "You are such a *Dwelbe* sometimes. You didn't hear that I had a hung jury. What you heard was that I had a *well*- hung jury."

And with that, the story ends. I am Enadious. Peace and prosperity to all.

EMBRYONIC
BY PERSEPHANIE CERDA

Lush gardens of green bend through her mind, twisting like orbital spheres; converging in listless abandon. Lynn's vision is coursing through prismatic symphonies as the fluid enters her lungs, surging into a bliss which she has never known before. The pink, fluidized sauce brings peace and vitality like morning dew upon blades of grass.

Muffled voices converge outside of the womb; hallow yet excited.

Lynn's body twists as the tubes inside the sack bind her. She is trying to see through the milky pink, trying to make out her captors. Weightless, she struggles to find footing, pleads with her body to react. Like grinding metal, shrill and screeching, they laugh outside the membrane, pointing long, disfigured fingers.

She tries to speak. The noises her mouth makes can only be heard within her own head.

A memory emerges: Thousands of ships landing in the distance. Millions of slouching people led to the vessels like sheep. She can hear a child whimper in the distance. A man screams in horror before being beaten down. A woman yells as her child is ripped from her grasp. Some are bleeding. Some are crying. Some wish they were dead.

Shrill voices commanding, pushing out un-interpretable orders with weapons held at shoulder level. Someone tries to run; the woman falls dead to the ground, a smoldering hole where her spine used to be. Lynn remembers gasping.

She steps over a body, mangled and broken. Bits of rib pierce dead flesh and charred skin. Those who fought back are now memories. Covered in filth, a baby cries on the ground. Thunder claps in the distance and another ship appears through the clouds, descending through the atmosphere like something concocted out of nightmares.

Rain pelts Lynn's face, stings her eyes, making it imposable to see. Through the cloud of moisture, she sees another person run. An explosive blast erupts and the mans arm vanishes in a cloud of sparks. Bits of meat fly from the husk of an arm, sailing off and slapping to the ground in tiny wet thuds.

161

She closes her eyes, wishing away the scene that refuses to be anything but real. These creatures bring death and misery. They laugh at the torment they inflict. Their objective seems to be pain.

In white suits, they came like angels to save the masses from impending doom. They said we would be safe. They spoke to us in our own tongues. Now their voices gurgle out like drowning beasts as they shuffle us aboard frightening ships that resemble cockroaches dipped in molten rock.

Lynn's memory fades.

She drifts back into reality, back into the membrane that encompasses her like plastic in a pool. Her breath is labored as the pink fluid fills her lungs like syrup, flowing down her throat in gulps that make her want to wretch. Forcing it down, she decides that it is the only thing keeping her alive.

The sack tightens around her, pressing firmly against her face, spreading thinly over her eyes. Lynn begins to see her surroundings; darkness gives way to faint illumination, clarifying the series of conveyors that the body bags are attached to, rising from the small vessels and into the inner workings of a much larger ship. Miles deep, the craft exposes millions of bags just like hers that carry those who happened to survive. Many struggle within their flexible prisons, desperately trying to move their arms and legs. Writhing body bags ascend into a portal at the very top of a platform, hundreds of feet above the main deck.

Lynn remembers being led to the door as one of the creatures slid a rubbery substance over her legs. The material began to shift and move, to migrate up along her pelvis and swallow her torso before it grew over her face. She panicked as the air escaped her lungs, replaced by the fluid that felt as if it were seeping into her pours. In a sudden rush, the fluid began to sustain her. Lynn relaxed.

Now, through the thin sack, Lynn watches as one of her neighbors flails within the membrane. Something sharp, like keys or a pocket knife protrudes through and tears the sack open. She watches as the woman dangles from the remnants of dripping fluid and ruptured tissue. The lady begins to slip when her grip loosens. Slime, pink and translucent smears across the skin sack until the woman falls. In a flash, she is gone, swallowed whole by the darkness below.

The tiny portal grows as Lynn gets closer. A beautiful white light radiates from within, pulsing like a firefly in the darkness. She tries to close her eyes, but the membrane restricts her eyelids. She is forced to watch as she is drawn closer to the end.

Lynn tries to think of fields of flowers, of beautiful grasses that lay beyond the passage. She wishes it were true as she hears the muffled cries of those who have already reached the other side. Her pulse quickens as she realizes that she is four bodies away from entering the unknown.

Sunflowers, daisies, lilies. . . she thinks as she draws near.

Children laughing, running through tall grass toward a tree. . . she prays.

The man in front of her flails, desperately trying to free himself. Lynn wonders what he sees that has him so afraid. She wonders what could be so terrifying that makes falling into the blackness below seem better than what is beyond the void.

Lynn returns to her dream. . . *The children begin to climb the massive Oak, reaching up to the lower branches. Their laughs are infectious. They scream like they are having the time of their life.*

Pop.

The mechanism that holds the man to the conveyor lets go. With a faint whoosh, he falls away from sight. His muffled voice slips away into nothingness. They conveyor only stops for a second before jerking forward once again. Lynn tries to hold her breath, but a rush of fluid spews into her mouth and nose, shocking her back to her senses.

Click. . . the conveyor stops.

Pop.

The children are falling from the branches; one flailing body at a time.

Falling. Weightless and soaring as if she were in flight. She wishes that she could feel the wind licking at her hair. If anything, she yearns for that small reprieve.

Impact.

Lynn feels the bodies writhe beneath her. Encased limbs reach out as far as the membrane will allow. Someone falls on top of her and she whimpers. Her body is jostled around. She can clearly see what is happening.

Below, a sea of corpses digest in green fluid. Bones poke out of the acidic mixture, melting slowly before receding into soup. Flesh sizzles. As the membrane melts away, she can hear the shrill screams of man and woman and child; crying, yelling, pleading for their lives.

"It burns!" a child exclaims before becoming swallowed by the digestive fluids, its voice becomes slurred by its burning tongue.

Lynn feels a distinct sensation. A tingle runs along the skin of her left foot. Her flesh tightens as the pain begins. She winces as the fluid laps at her leg, slowly melting away the nerve endings, inch by inch.

The children are being swallowed by the earth, devoured by the soil.

Another body lands on top of Lynn, but she doesn't feel the impact. All she can feel is the acid rip away her skin as she hears engines ignite in the background. With a thunderous whoosh, the acids begin to recede, stoking the fires that full the massive ships.

IN THE COURT OF CRIMSON KING
BY GEOFFERY CRESCENT

They came and they saw and they didn't exactly conquer, but what they did give us was the technology to move forward in time. Tiny jumps at first, just to test the water. Five minutes until your favorite TV show, jump it forward. Waiting for the kettle to boil, jump it forward. Those last crawling moments of the working day, jump it forward.

Of course it wasn't long before people started asking questions. Like what exactly happened in those intervening moments when you were jumping. For all intents and purposes to those around you, you appeared exactly the same. Carrying on with your menial, day to day tasks with perhaps only a slightly blank expression in those longer jumps to betray you. But your mind was racing, racing forward to the time of your arrival, without pause or recollection. It wasn't so much technology, although that was there too in the form of two tiny chips, one in your index finger and one in your temple. Match the two together and you could jump forward as far as you like. But technology was only half the procedure; only by focusing correctly on your time of arrival could you jump properly. There were people who could only manage minute trips, there was one half-baked story about a man so nervous about proposing to his girlfriend in a few days' time he decided to jump forward to just before the main event, and instead ended up overshooting it and found himself sitting outside his apartment on a pile of black bins full of clothes because she'd refused. Another more visceral tale was of a half-controlled jump, the man in question was still aware of all his movements, travelling as if at top speed, and sensing his heart rate increase exponentially suffered a heart attack.

But horror stories could do nothing to the popularity of a contrivance that made life so much easier and more bearable because you could just skim over the more boring and repetitive aspects of your life. Soon people were making longer and longer jumps, and the regulations were brought in. No jumping to avoid exams or tests. No jumping whilst driving. No jumping on public transport. All this

165

seemed pretty perfunctory at first; because when you jumped you just did exactly the same things you did normally, except that you weren't aware of them. In fact studies showed that people actually performed better in tests because their subconscious was open and all that information which usually stays stuffed at the back of your mind came floating to the surface. And then there were the addicts, people so enamored of jumping that it was all they could do to live life at normal speed. Threatened with counseling or the forcible removal of their chips, a scarred temple became as much a sign of weakness as lying in the gutter with a bottle. But we stuck to the rules and carried on with our lives in much the same way as before. At least, that was until someone got killed.

The biggest problem was, of course, that it was just so hard to tell when people were jumping. There was that vague, empty expression that some people carried, but any expression can be feigned easily enough. Then there was the internal counter that logged the time and duration of each jump, but these could be reset as easily as a phone inbox, and for much the same reasons. Who would want their partner to find out they'd jumped through a night of passion? King claimed to have jumped throughout the whole affair, but with his logs empty and a whole body of evidence pointing toward him, he was brought to trial in the company of both the court and our alien benefactors, the Delirium.

They'd come upon us one day three years ago, not like rain water on parched crops but like a subtle upgrade to an already advanced product. At first innovative, improving our lives in so many small ways, but later slipping quietly out of focus, out of sight and then there were few who remained on our planet. It wasn't just jumping, but new medical technologies, cleaner fuels, new crops, nothing that our own scientists hadn't already conceived but could never hope to achieve in their own lifetimes. The Delirium brought all of that, and asked nothing for return but their own sanctuary should they ask of it.

But from the few who remained here, like celebrity icons and living conversation pieces, came the strangest of jurors and judges. To each a unique double helix like living rock, each a singular pearlescent shade, but for the strangely cruel yellow beak and lidless eyes on stalks that protruded from their shrouded cloaks like the eyes of a crab. The court was formed, half human, half alien, a high profile case to which camera crews and curious onlookers flocked like flies to a turd. At stake not just the fate of King, but of jumping itself, for a technology that allowed atrocities such as this to take place would be swiftly withdrawn, to find only a new home on the black market. King himself was represented by a human lawyer, in an attempt to claim the technology itself had forced him into the murder. His prosecution, on the other hand, a Delirium who saw his own people threatened by claims that jumping was dangerous. By extension, so was he.

King entered the courtroom flanked by burly police officers, his hands bound not by shackles, but by shimmering loops of light that weaved inexorably between them. Yet another helping hand from our alien benefactors. As he ascended the steps to the dock he was met with a mixture of cheers and cat-calls, his case proving almost completely divisive. The court rose for the arrival of Judge Gibson; an alien judge was presumed to be too biased and it seemed only fair that King was tried by a member of his own species.

And so the proceedings went forth as much as any traditional court hearing, but for the presence of the opalescent aliens in the crowd, in the prosecution and even in the public audience, their glimmering presence going almost unnoticed amongst the sober affair. It was becoming more and more clear, however, there was more to the case than the simple question of whether or not King was under the influence.

First, the alien presented his attack on King. It was a more curious facet of the aliens' behavior that while they had quickly learned to adopt our speech and mannerisms, they refused to take on human names as they had our culture. Hence the prosecution was referred to as Del#44S. He swept to the front of the bench, his loose cotton robe looking altogether too casual amongst the suits and smartness of the congregation and but confidently setting himself apart and above them all.

"I have a question very simply put for you, Mister Crimson."

"King."

"I'm sorry."

"My name's King, call me King."

King who had, until now, been slumped over the edge of the dock displaying apparent apathy, raised his head to face Del#44S. He had a thin sallow face, his pale red hair fell long down his back and into his eyes. He pushed it resolutely off his forehead and attempted to look directly at his accuser, a difficult feat considering the Delirium stood a good three feet taller than the average human, and their eyes were located somewhere around their waist. King settled for staring directly at the twisted horn facing him as Del#44S continued.

"Your name is Mister Crimson is it not? It would be rude surely of me to call you by so colloquial a term."

Judge Gibson interrupted, "This is hardly relevant to the case. Just call him King."

Del#44S shifted stance slightly, his eyes twisting to face his own body. "No."

Gibson looked utterly dumbfounded as the alien continued his questioning.

"So Mister Crimson is it true that you were jumping whilst you committed the murder?"

"Yes."

Del#44S slowly elongated his eye stalks back to face King in the dock. "Well I do not think that you were."

"I was."

"Well that's completely irrelevant. There is no evidence whatsoever that you were jumping on that night."

"I deleted my logs. I don't like them to get clogged up."

"The fact is Mister Crimson that you did not delete your logs because there was no log. You simply went outside, with a knife and butchered a poor old man that you did not even know…"

"Er…I did know him."

"I am sorry?" The alien performed a strange sort of pirouette at this apparently startling piece of news.

King stood a little straighter in the dock, sensing he'd gained an advantage. "Yeah, he goes to the same pub as me. Always asking for money for drinks. Owed me about thirty quid. I did mention that in my opening statement," he added to Gibson.

Indeed. Please continue." He motioned to the alien.

"So!" Del#44S's eyes were now standing straight up as if electrocuted, seemingly focusing on an air vent in the ceiling. "This man owed you money! So you thought you'd kill him and take it!"

"No! Why would I kill him? I just said he never had any money on him. I knew he'd pay me eventually, he was just some cheap old bloke from the pub. I didn't want to kill him."

"Hmm..." Del#44S appeared to be digesting this information. "Incidentally, what pub was this that you both did frequent?"

"The Dogtooth."

"Hmm... and do they serve Thatcher's Gold there?"

"What?"

"Thatcher's Gold. Do they serve that beverage there?'

"What? I don't...what has this got to do with anything?"

"I was only asking!"

"Objection your Honor!" This now from King's defense Tilby, a wiry, nervous looking man who had spent the majority of the case tugging at his collar and opening and shutting his briefcase. His dislike for the Delirium was clear, cringing each time one glided past him. "This has nothing to do with the case!"

"I agree. Could you please stick to the subject at hand?" asked Gibson.

"I was merely gathering some background information," said Del#44S, sounding rather affronted. He said nothing more for a few minutes, only his eyes whirring and twisting about themselves gave any indication that he was doing anything at all, and was not just silent rock. An irritated cough from Tilby appeared to shake him out of this reverie.

"Is it true Mister Crimson that you are a jumping addict?" he asked suddenly.

"I, well I've been treated for that in the past, I'm not anymore," replied King.

"So you refrain from jumping at all costs? Therefore making it ABSOLUTELY CERTAIN," he roared the last two words, flecks of luminous spittle flying from his beak, "that you were not jumping on the night of the murder! You just walked straight out of your door, ran into a poor old man and stabbed him in cold blood because he owed you thirty pounds. You murderer! You foul cretin! You... you." He fished about for a more appropriate insult. "You cheeky bastard!"

"That will do!" thundered Gibson. "Have you anything to say?" he added softly to King.

King was now slumped back in the dock, head drooping as if rather tired of the proceedings. "I still jump. I'm just keeping it under better control now."

"Aha, so you do still jump! So you were jumping that night!"

King was confused. "Yes, that's what I've been saying all along. You're the one who's trying to prove me wrong!"

"Right. Yes." Del#44S performed another of those odd pirouettes, but slowly this time. As he faced the back of the court his eyes came to rest on another Delirium sitting in the audience. He gave a slight nod to Del#44S, who turned back to face Judge Gibson.

"No further questions your Honor." He swept slowly and silently back to his seat. Tilby launched himself from his seat as the alien approached, and began pacing nervously back and forth in front of the docks until Del#44S was seated and Gibson nodded to him that he could begin. He continued to pace swiftly as he talked, his tattered suit looking more likely to break at the seams with each step he took.

"So King. We've already established that you, despite being a former addict, have now recovered and make frequent jumps, am I correct?"

"Well." King pondered this for a bit. "I wouldn't say frequent. But yes you're correct."

"And on the night in question you were jumping? Why exactly?"

"I was only waiting for my dinner to cook in the oven. Took about half an hour, nothing else to do, so I jumped it."

"You weren't planning on taking a walk then?"

"No. As I said, just waiting for my dinner to cook."

"Using a kitchen knife?"

"Well yeah, but I put it in the sink afterwards, I didn't go walking around with it."

"And what was your relationship with Mister Cottle like?"

"S'okay I suppose. Just some bloke from the pub. Liked the Bee Gees. I don't know, look, he was just a guy I knew, I didn't want to kill him!"

"And which pub was this again?"

"The Dogtooth."

"Ah yes. And do they serve Black Sheep there?"

"I'm not answering that!"

"Of course not,' said Gibson. 'Continue please Mister Tilby."

"So you wouldn't have killed him even though he owed you thirty pounds?"

"No! Who does that?"

"But perhaps in the back of your mind, you did want to kill him. I mean." He faced the audience. "We've all felt that from time to time haven't we? Just wanted to kill someone because they annoy us? Maybe the tech picked up on that and took you to kill Mister Cottle while you were jumping. The default action, as it were."

"I don't know! I just know I didn't want to kill him."

"King." Tilby looked him in the eye. "Maybe you did and." Here he carefully enunciated every word. "The-tech-picked-up-on-this. This-is-the-point-we're-trying-to-make."

King caught on. "Right. Well maybe subconsciously, but I'd never do it for real!"

"Yes, yes." Tilby smiled benignly. "Who would blame you? I mean he was," and he whispered the last word, "black."

"I'm sorry?" asked Gibson

"I said he was black," said Tilby, a little more loudly but still obviously aware of the implications this statement carried.

"Don't be so ridiculous!" cried King. "I'm not a racist! I didn't mean to kill him and even if I had wanted to kill him, it wouldn't have been because of that!"

"So you are admitting there were other motives to your murdering him?"

"What? No, I didn't murder him, whose side are you meant to be on here?"

"Apparently on the side of the white supremacists,' interjected Gibson, giving Tilby a hard look. "Court is adjourned."

The court began to file out, first the Judge, followed by the jurors and finally the crowd, the humans shuffling footsteps interspersed with the soft gliding of the Delirium. The aliens congregated together in a corner of the hallway, saying nothing but holding their eyes out in a circle so that each one was stuck to the one next to it. They stood like this for a while, gently swaying. Then their eyes came free with a sticky, squelching sound. As one they murmured, "Yes."

Tilby had run hurriedly after King, who was still flanked by his guards; all three seemed fairly at ease, but for King's glowing shackles.

"Well I think that went rather well don't you?" smiled Tilby.

King smiled back at him. "Shove off. Racist prick," he said, still smiling. Tilby nodded nervously to the policemen, neither of whom acknowledged him. He shuffled back toward the door of the court, and leant against the wall, waiting.

By the time the court came back in session, there was a tangible change in the atmosphere. The air seemed to crackle with electricity, and while the people seemed no more excited than before, the Delirium seemed to glow with an evanescent light. As everyone trooped back to their seats they made their way, as a group, to the front of the dock and stood there silently until Judge Gibson had entered. He balked a little at their sudden gathering.

"It's okay, you can take your seat," said Del#44S brightly.

"I...thank you?" said Gibson, ascending to his rightful place above the assembled crowd. "Now..." he began, but Del#44S interrupted him. "Oh no, we are talking now. Sssh!"

Gibson spluttered a little, but did fall silent as the alien continued.

"Now where are we? Yes, Del#7749 would you like to continue?"

"Pleasured to," replied Del#7749. He was taller even than his companions, a deep, pulsing cherry red in color. "I think at this point in the proceedings we will have to take charge. Now we came here to your planet and you have shown us nothing but gratitude and appreciation. Well, nearly all of you have anyway," he added with a sideways glance at Tilby, who was squirming in his seat like a deranged ferret. Del#7749 continued, "We gave you our technology, not just to jump, but to heal, to cleanse, to transport and you took it all at face value and never once did you ask why. Why we were giving this to you? Because we're *nice aliens* and we just give you stuff because you let us stay on your little planet? Did you not think it was strange?"

Gibson cleared his throat as if about to answer but Del#7749 shot across him. "We don't want you to answer! We want you to listen! For once people just shut up and listen! You will find that by now, none of that technology will work anymore."

Almost as one the assembled people lifted their index finger to their temples in an attempt to jump. As one they repeatedly stabbed at their foreheads and gazed at each other in confusion and then horrified realization at what had just been taken away from them. King meanwhile had suddenly noticed that there were no longer any manacles around his wrists. Del#44S jerked an eye at him.

"You are 'off the hook' as they say. Go on, go."

In the Court of Crimson King

Needing no further encouragement King took off at top speed past the milling crowds, through the court room doors and across town to the Dogtooth, which served a fine selection of beverages and where he knew he would be welcomed. Back in the courtroom the humans were beginning to get restless, a brave few even getting to their feet to shake an angry fist at the Delirium. But the silky glow that surrounded them was surging outward and upward, forming an impenetrable barrier between them and the people.

"The time has come!" shouted Del#7749 silencing the disgruntled shouts. "The walrus said," he added to a soft giggle from his companions. "I'm telling you now why we decided to bestow these gifts upon you. Perhaps you thought yourselves special, that the aliens had singled you out and given you lots of lovely toys. But you were wrong. You were merely test subjects in a much larger game than you could possibly imagine."

A shocked silence filled the room as the alien continued. "You see, before we introduce any new technology to our own people, we have to do a test run on a lesser species. Oh, do not act so shocked!" he spat. "Do you do any different to the animals you test your piffling commodities on? There was a slight chance that jumping, whilst maintaining a state of unconscious consciousness in the user, would drag up base desires and needs and urges from the back of the mind. Only a tiny percentage mind, but it just was not worth the risk. And as I am sure you realize by now, we were right. The technology was flawed. But do not worry; I think we have put you through enough for now. We will test the readjustments on another useless planet. We will be taking our leave of you now."

A soft hum began to fill the still stunned silence. "Mind you, I will miss Pringles," muttered Del#7749 to a companion. "I always liked them."

"You…you're not going to kill us all then?" asked the voice of Tilby from somewhere beneath his table.

"Well if we were going to kill anyone it would be you," said Del#44S matter-of-factly. "Racist tosser," he added. "But no, there is just no sense in it. It would take your planet far too long to readjust and produce another species of relatively intelligent life and we may want to test another product on you before then."

The humming had reached a loud crescendo. The Delirium

matched their eyes together a second time, and gradually faded from the view of the courtroom. The hum died away and the light dimmed, leaving no evidence that the aliens had ever been there at all. And the congregation stared at each other in horror, not because they had been deceived and not mourning for their loss but at the thought of all those hours they would now have to fill.

THE COMET CHASERS
BY JOHN MCCUAIG

"Good, that's it. Get right on its tail my boy." Captain Jeff Jones placed a reassuring hand on the shoulder of his nervous young pilot. "You're doing just fine. Once we get inside the slipstream the ride will get a whole lot smoother."

All six crew members of the survey ship, Excalibur, were busy in their work during the final approach to Comet XJ-109. They didn't seem to worry, or care, that the ship was being buffeted around from side to side as it chased after its target at over 20,000 miles per hour. Inside the large glass sphere which housed the bridge they could see a full 360 degrees around. The photo sensitive glass was forever changing its tints and hues so that the crew could see every single detail of what was happening outside, all of which was set to the exact same brightness.

"'Temperature and radiation levels are all still within safety limits Captain," announced Eric McLean, the ships second-in-command. He spoke as he tapped away on the keyboard of his computer while his eyes remained firmly stuck to the screen. Jones went back and sat down on his chair; as he watched his crew expertly handle their tasks he almost relaxed. Almost being the most important word for he knew that this was no ordinary comet. Whatever it was, it wasn't just a great big ball of ice and dirt like all the others.

It was over five years ago that the first pictures of XJ-109 were taken by the Hubble Space Telescope. They showed the wondrous aura of every light of the rainbow shimmer around its hazy half mile long body and the breathtaking bursts of colors which flew off in all directions every few minutes. No one knew then, or indeed now, what caused it but as there were so many guesses and notions being banded around this mission was born. The comet, named Artemis after the Greek goddess of light, would come so close to Earth that for a few days and nights every man, woman and child on the planet would be able to watch its journey across the sky. Before it arrived we needed to know more about it.

The vibrations coming through the transparent floor slowly

ceased and this signaled to Jones the first part of the mission had been completed. As he stood back up, he felt as though he could almost reach out through the glass and touch the lights.

"Okay folks, let's get all those fancy gadgets to work, find out everything you can, please." The Captain may have come from a scientific background himself, but he knew that his crews' knowledge far out weighed his own. So for this trip at least he was happy to leave it all to them.

As Excalibur eased itself closer and closer to Artemis, almost like a moth to a flame, Captain Jones walked around the glass dome and watched the merry dance of the colors that were now just a few hundred feet away outside. Once he got to the front of the dome his eyes became transfixed on the blurred image of the main body of Artemis as it slowly came into view. By what seemed like only inches it got closer and the captain lost him self deep in its wondrous beauty. That was until the new view shocked him back to reality.

"Someone please confirm what I am seeing." He only got silence in return. "Come on people! You've got billions of pounds worth of sensors pointed at this thing, but still, my own eyes can see it first!" Turning angrily around to face his crew he saw that they had shock imbedded deep in their faces. Jones guessed that those fancy instruments were indeed showing the same as his eyes.

Spinning back he found it was already filling up the whole view of the horizon. It was almost unbelievable; a massive, but perfectly round and perfectly white ball was at the heart of Artemis.

"Helm, keep your distance for now, don't get us too close." His eyes remained transfixed ahead so he shouted without turning. "McLean. I need to know what the hell we are dealing with."

The pilot slowed Excalibur quickly to match speed with Artemis and the distance between them stayed constant giving the four scientists some time to get to work. They all seem to speak at once and their voices rose and rose as they fought each other to put their own views across. It was like each new idea needed to be louder than the other. Throughout this time, Jones could not take his eyes off the football stadium sized white ball which now seemed to be floating directly in front of his ship. Whatever this was, it obviously was not a natural phenomenon.

"Captain," a puzzled sounding McLean piped up. "All our scans are just bouncing back off it, we can get info on its size and speed, but we haven't a clue what it's made from. We're trying to adjust the scanners, but we're going to need some more time."

The captain did not like that answer. "Helm, get me through to Mission Control, we're going to need some help on this. Also, I want to know what the hell they'll want us to do next."

The pilot, Andy Banstead, nervously answered, "Can't do that sir. Now that we are inside its magnetic field we can't send any signals out. We'll have to leave to call home."

Jones, who was slightly angry with himself as he should have known that, tried to weigh up the pros and cons of what to do next. If they were to leave he had to take into account the risks of the maneuvers out of the field and then no doubt having to come back in again to continue the mission. It doesn't take him long to come to his decision.

"You've got thirty minutes people. We don't seem to be in any danger for the moment, so let's use that time to get me some information. When that time is up, it's up, and we leave for Mission Control." All four of the scientists looked up for a second, nodded, then just as quickly got back to their computers and got back to work.

After about ten minutes, Carla Vialli was the first to speak out, "Captain, I need you over here straight away." Dragging himself away from the almost hypnotic views outside, she had started talking before he even got within ten feet. "It's the lights, sir, whilst doing the scans I've noticed how they're lapping all over the body of our ship. At first I thought it was just random, but then I saw there was a pattern. They are going over every inch of the ship in a few seconds and then they start it over and over again. If I had to make a guess I would say it was scanning us."

Looking all over the full 360 degrees of the dome, he watched the red, yellow and blue streaks race over the ship; his ship. "How the hell can light scan us?" he questioned Vialli. She was still tapping away on her computer when she answered. "It's a theoretical idea that has been talked about for quite a while, sir. You see light reacts differently to every single object it touches; think about shining torch-light on water and then on wood- the same source, but the reflections are so different. This can translate to everything, the changes might be incredibly minute, but with good enough equipment to pick it up and enough source data it can actually be quite perfect."

Jones once again faced the body of Artemis. "So if it's reading us, scanning us, that proves there is a high intelligence at work here? It's learning all about us and we are still blindly just looking at it. Well that's enough for me. Mr. Banstead, start to back us away slowly son. Let's get out of here nice and easy." He once more sat back down on his comforting chair.

They heard the engine roar increase as the ship pushed itself against the magnetic field, Jones waited to see Artemis slip away into the distance, but it stayed the exact same size. "Banstead what's the problem? Why aren't we moving away?"

"Not sure, sir. Engines are at fifty percent, but there is no change in velocity. We are still exactly matching Artemis in both speed and direction."

"Give it all you've got lad. Just get us out of here."

Excalibur vibrated wildly as the engines were put beyond their max, but thanks to the wonderful views from inside the sphere the crew could plainly see they were not moving anywhere. Artemis still sat proud and bright, and directly ahead of them.

"Cut the engines," Jones muttered. "We aren't going to get away from here with raw power." He studied Artemis before speaking up again. "Okay, it's time for you scientists to get your brains in gear and come up with something clever; lets get to work on finding us a solution."

They didn't have any time, within a matter of seconds of the engines being pulled back, Artemis moved toward them and in a flash; it was only a matter of feet outside the glass. Its huge size filled the view from almost everywhere inside the dome. The intensity of the lights flared up so high the reactive glass couldn't keep track. The dome had great dark waves appearing where the light had burnt its surface permanently. Jones saw that while it may have only been a small portion of the glass at that moment, if it continued for a couple of hours, they would be blanked out completely. He looked again over at Artemis; he knew he couldn't let that happen.

"Help me out here people!" he barked. "We need to come up with an idea to get us out of here." He looked right at the scientists, but they were just staring back at him. "Come on, think. We can get through this if we don't panic and put our trust in science."

Ten minutes of shouting and screaming at each other had not brought the scientists any closer to a solution, but then it was Artemis itself that once again made them go quiet. The light show suddenly stopped; turning around as in one the whole crew looked toward the bow of their ship. Artemis had started glowing, it was no longer a pure white, instead there were slight tones of pinks and greens racing over its body. Then it fired the beam.

A bright pink, foot wide beam of light was being fired on the dome and it didn't take long for them to see why. "Captain," Vialli shouted. "It's cutting right through the glass. We are going to lose atmosphere any second!" The crew quickly put on their oxygen masks apart from Captain Jones; he just sat himself back down on his chair in the centre of the bridge. He knew that those little plastic masks were not going to be much use if they were treated to the vacuum and coldness of deep space. Dead in a matter of seconds is what they'd be.

Whoosh! The beam cut through the glass and rushed into the bridge, but it stayed at its foot wide diameter and didn't spread out. Vialli left her console and moved a couple of feet, but then it started to pull back until it reached the hole it made and stopped. "No loss of atmosphere, captain," she stated the obvious while closely inspecting the aperture. As her hand reached out dozens of small red beams flew out from the middle of the pink tube and after twisting through the air they swarmed all over Vialli, covering every inch of her body.

"Captain! Please help me!" she screamed while trying wildly to brush away the lights. As soon as Jones made a move toward her, another set of the pencil thin lights came rushing out and wrapped themselves around him. Within a couple of seconds he couldn't move a muscle as the beams held him steady in place as they seemed to survey his body. It was only his eyes that could move and they saw more of the beams arrive and wrap up tight the rest of his now panicked crew. Jones soon realized that he felt no pain at all from the beams, no heat or friction were burning his skin, whatever they were doing, for the time being, they were causing him no harm. Some of the beams left him and his crew and converged on the mass array of computers all over the bridge. In a flash they seemed to disappear deep inside the towers and memory banks while the screens and displays all burst into life. All the ships files flew across those screens so fast Jones could only see them as a blur.

Then they saw them arrive. Three small white orbs came out of the pink beam and grew four feet in diameter as soon as they were clear. The white glowing orbs were just like mini versions of Artemis itself.

Gliding effortlessly through the air, two of them went directly over to the computers while the other orb headed for Jones and stopped barely inches from his face. This one started to change color and then vivid red and green flashing started to dance across its smooth surface. The other two immediately joined in with this display, but Jones saw that they were also sending wispy waves of green light onto the computer banks. Then the speaker system throughout the ship cracked into life and in the artificial voice of the automated systems it began to boom out.

"By taking information from your vessel, we have learned your language, learned about you, and learned about your planet. We are travelers from a far distant world and are on our way through this galaxy mapping the stars and planets."

The orb by Jones went bright red for a split second and then the lights that were holding the captain still dissipated and he was set free from their hold.

Jones was at first speechless, but as he surveyed the madness around him he felt the need to speaks out. "Please, can you release the rest of my crew, it's clear that we are obviously no danger to you. Your technology is far superior to ours."

"You are of course no danger to us, but you can be a danger to yourselves. Your planet's history has shown us that you are unpredictable and liable to strike out at the unknown. I will do as you ask and release the others, but they must not interfere."

With another bright red flash off its surface all the holding beams disappeared and the other Excalibur crew members were then set free. Captain Jones held his hands up in the air. "People, don't move. Everyone just stay calm and don't do anything stupid. We are involved in dialogue with our visitors so please show me a bit of patience, lets give this some time." He looked at every one of his staff straight in the eye and waited for them to nod before moving onto the next. They all agreed and he then turned back to face the orb.

"Thank you. Thank you for showing us some trust. Now can you tell me how we can become friends?" The orbs flashed their lights back and forth to each other in what seemed a response to this question. He tried to push forward his case. "I'm sure you found out when checking our computers that we're all followers of science here, we're men and women of peace on this ship. We are like you; we have devoted our lives in the search of knowledge."

The flashing stopped.

The main orb moved away from Jones and stopped in the middle of the bridge. The electronically produced voice started up again.

"We find that some of what we have discovered and also what you have said may be of an interest to us for study. We shall return to your planet when we have finished our survey mission and then we will meet again to continue our discussions. We shall now leave. I, however, promise that we shall return."

By then, Jones didn't want them to leave. "Can't you stay for just a little longer. Our people back on Earth will want to hear a lot more about you and our meeting."

"No, we cannot. We have already delayed our mission enough. Time is paramount to us." The main orb then started to shrink in size to fit back down the beam.

"When?" Jones shouted out before it was too late. "When will you be coming back?"

The last orb stayed stationary for a second. *"In your timescale it will be approximately eleven years and two months."*

No more was heard and they quickly shrank and headed off down the beam. A bright white flash sealed the hole in the dome glass air tight and the beam fully retracted back into Artemis. Jones wondered about Artemis, was it a ship as we understand them? Were the smaller orbs living beings or were they some sort of probes? He also knew there was plenty of time for the world's scientists to argue about that.

A heavy lurch was felt as Artemis released Excalibur from its mighty grasp. The fantastic sight of it soon propelled away into the distance and all they were left with was that hazy colorful sight which they first saw so many hours ago.

"Captain," McLean whispered as he walked over to stand by Jones. "Do you think they will come back?"

"I'm sure they will, Ian, I'm sure they will. They didn't seem like the lying type to me." The two men looked at each other and exchanged a little smile.

Andy Banstead was the next to speak with his youthful nervousness showing through in his voice. "How do you think the people back home will react when they know that the fancy light they see up in the sky is actually a ship full of aliens? It's going to send people mad and will they have the patience to wait so many years for them to return?"

"I have no idea, son. But I do know it's certainly going to cause a wee bit of a stir." Jones took a long deep breath and sat back down again in his comforting chair. "Well, I suppose I'd better get the ball rolling now that we're in the clear."

He pointed his finger toward Banstead and then over to his station at the con. "Okay, Helm, please patch me through to Mission Control, I've got a little story to tell them."

UNDEAD SIDE OF THE MOON
BY LYLE PEREZ-TINICS

To Whom It May Concern:

My name is Elroy Collins and I'm sitting in a prison cell awaiting punishment for what I'm being accused of. I'm writing this to prove my innocence, but the trial is over; I am convicted of murdering my team and every resident at the Moonlit Resort. The only thing left for me to do is to write down my side of the story. Maybe someday, this letter will inform people that the Zilith Corporations was lying.

* * *

We needed to learn to take care of planet Earth before we went off building in outer space. I was against opening the Moonlit Resort for business so soon, but the Zilith Corporation wouldn't listen. Why would they listen to a roughneck like me? I was just head of their secret search and rescue team; no one important.

In 2036 the Zilith Corporation was responsible for the Apophis asteroid impact. By this time, NASA had lost all funding because space exploration was becoming more popular with privately funded organizations. After NASA disbanded, the Zilith Corporation caused an unnecessary public scare, saying that NASA had it wrong and that the asteroid *was* on a collision course with Earth, the United States Government allowed them to shift the asteroid's orbit in order to make the near Earth object hit the moon. It was a successful impact. The entire world stood watch as Apophis collided with our moon. I was only fifteen years old, but I remember it well. In fact, watching it changed my life. It was at that time that I fell in love with space travel and wanted to do anything I could to become a Space Marshall. The impact made a small explosion on the surface of the moon. A few minutes after the flare-up, dust ejected into space causing a brilliant light show. After the collision was over and the raves to the Zilith Corporation for saving the world stopped, people went back to their lives. Just like the moon landings in 1969. Once the United States beat Russia in the Space Race, people lost interest in the moon.

Five years after the Apophis collision, in 2041, the Zilith Corporation revealed their plan to build a multi-trillion dollar resort on the surface of the moon. Thanks to the asteroid, they had more than enough raw materials waiting for them. The dust still had not settled from the impact, but advances in nano-technology and the space exploration boom of the 2020's, made space walking safer than ever. Not to mention all the scientific breakthroughs of that decade as well. Radiation repelling space suits that could withstand heat greater than 1,000 degrees Fahrenheit made it possible for explorers to go places they'd never gone before, but oxygen levels were still a problem. Zilith was on it, bioengineering artificial lung mechanisms that made breathing in space possible, and they were just a step away from surgically implanting their invention into a handful of human test subjects. Don't ask me about specifics, I'm no scientist. Till this day, I still have not heard of any success stories.

Despite the rough shape the Apophis collision left the moon, Zilith Corporation managed to fully erect the first lunar hotel on the northern part of the moon in only seven years. World scientists agreed it was an ideal location for building, and by 2048, the hotel was completed. Just like with the Apophis collision, people were glued to their E-vision sets as Zilith streamed live video and photos during building construction.

I had been recruited and working security for Zilith nearly two years by the time construction was completed. Zilith is not the type of company you go to find work, if they like your achievements, they find you. I was stunned when a recruiter met me at my graduation. I finished first in my Space Marshall training class and was ready for work. Upon my first day of employment, I had a team ready for me to oversee.

They claimed that no one died in the processes of making the building, but I know the truth. Zilith does a wonderful job keeping everything in the dark. I lost two good friends who were on the moon building project. They hit an air pocket while digging and were ejected into space. The man in charge of the dig told me that before he mysteriously died from natural causes. The official story was that they went insane and killed themselves. Their faces were so badly disfigured that the funeral was closed casket. I'm not sure what they put in those coffins, but it wasn't their remains.

The doors to Moonlit Resort remained closed for the next five years, while Zilith tested the safety and stability of the hotel. When the doors finally opened in 2053, the rooms were fully-booked for the first four years. A one night stay is a flat rate of one-million a head, plus an additional fifty-grand for the lunar shuttle ride each way. Needless to say, the only people traveling to the moon were the wealthy.

Everything was going great until we lost communication with them a few weeks ago. From here on out I will be telling the true story of what really took place.

* * *

We lost communication with the Moonlit Resort on December 28, 2059. The shuttle rides had stopped until we could regain contact. The communications team went to check how the resort was doing, but there was no response. It was dead silent. For an entire week after, they tried to restore communication, but were unsuccessful. The Zilith Corporation kept the lid on tight until more information was known. After many attempts to reach the hotel, my team and I had orders to take an immediate flight to see what happened. I didn't understand it at the time, there was no reason to send armed space officers. There were already security guards at the hotel. I was certain it was just an antenna malfunction and a construction crew could handle it. It wasn't like we received a distress call or anything. We hoped for a simple antenna failure on their end, but we planned for the worst.

"Space Marshal Collins," I heard someone say as I packed my bag with clothing and equipment. I turned and standing in front of me was, Mr. Sam Wallace. He was my direct line to the big wigs at Zilith Corp. If I had something to say to them, I told Mr. Wallace and he re-layed the message.

"Sir?" I looked into his dark eyes. His white hair was messier than normal and he looked stressed. His tie was loosened around his neck and the top button of his shirt was undone.

"I have a message for you from the bosses," he paused and took a note out of his inside coat pocket. He handed it to me and said, "That's all and good luck on your venture." He stuck out his hand and we shook.

"Thanks, Sam," I said quite informal as we let go. He turned and walked out of the room.

I opened the message and it read,

Space Marshal Collins

Keep this investigation under wraps. You or your team may not have any contact with family or friends during this mission or until debriefing upon your return. There will be dire consequences if you violate this agreement. Be safe and report back to Mr. Wallace within four days. Thank you for your loyalty to the company.

Zilith Corporation

I put the note in my back pocket and continued packing. I flung the sack over my shoulder and headed toward my team's room.

"Space Marshal. Ten-hut!" Mick said. The four other men in the room quickly stood at attention.

"At ease," I replied. I never liked it when my men greeted me that way. They were not just my men, they were my friends. "Are you guys ready?" I asked, looking around the room.

To the far left was Patrick Swan, the pilot in charge of getting us there and back safely. He stood wringing his hands out in front of him. His sack was closed and sitting on the chair next to him.

Next to Patrick was Mick Greenwell, my second in command and the deadliest shot with an S-801 Rifle. He stared back with his long black hair tied in a ponytail. His sack was closed along with his gun cases.

In the middle, John Megs stood. He was the communications specialist I wanted to take with me in case the antenna needed tweaking. We have taken him with us on different missions to Moonlit Resort. We already considered him part of the team even though, officially, he was not.

Standing to the right, still packing, were the two brothers, Orlando and Austin Flint. Their job was to keep the fire power going in case we were met with an attack.

I looked at Orlando and Austin, "You got five minutes to finish packing. The rest of you head for the spacecraft. John, start your check and get us ready for flight."

The men nodded and filed out of the room.

Spacecrafts were very different than the ones they used pre-2020. Rocket science was also mastered within that decade. The spacecrafts were much smaller and looked like oversized F-16 fighter jets. It took the Apollo missions three days to reach the moon. The Zilith Corp. managed to reach it in approximately 22 hours.

Orlando, Austin and I walked into the spacecraft. John and Mick were already strapped in. Patrick was at the control panels getting the craft ready for flight. I took a seat next to him while Orlando and Austin tied our packs and weapons in the storage containers then took seats.

The weapons we took to space weren't that different than the ones we used on Earth. Bullets must be exploded out of their casing, but in order for it to fire, there needs to be oxygen present. But there is no oxygen in space. The casing we use as slightly bigger in order to entrap more oxidizer into the casing. The explosion uses that to fire the bullet. One cool thing about guns is that they will fire faster and better in space than on Earth because there is less atmospheric pressure.

"Mission control this is Shadow Three, copy," Patrick said. "We are ready for flight. Please clear the runway. Over."

There was a pause.

"Copy, Shadow Three, I don't see you on the departure list. Who authorized a space flight for today? Over."

Patrick looked at me and said, "Does anyone know about our mission?"

"Not many," I answered back and took over the microphone. "Mission Control, this is Shadow One, copy? Over."

"Copy Shadow One, who authorized? Over."

"Mission Control, this is a black operation. Contact Sam Wallace if you have a problem. Over." I answered.

There was another pause.

"Shadow One, you're clear for take off. Clearing runway. Over."

"Thank you, Mission Control. Shadow One over and out." I said.

The other spacecrafts on the runway cleared quickly. There was ten miles of open runway space. I looked back at my team, who were holding on to their seats. Take off was always the worst part about the trip. Seeing those big men terrified of the flight was almost comical.

Patrick began the countdown. "Powering up in three, two, one," he said as he turned on the first thruster. The aircraft began to move forward slowly. "Firing thruster two in three, two, one." He flipped the switch for thruster two. The spacecraft jolted forward at one-hundred miles an hour.

"Ah shit," someone in the back yelled.

I held on to my seat as Patrick began talking again. "Firing thruster three in, three, two, one. Hold on," he said as he pushed the third thruster.

The spacecraft progressed forward nearly reaching three hundred miles an hour. The runway was running out of space.

Patrick held on to the steering controls and yelled, "Here we go!" Pre-2020 spacecrafts were nothing more than a rocket that moves in one direction. The spacecraft we used could be steered, no matter where you were. He pulled back on the handles and the spacecraft lifted into the air at three hundred miles an hour. "Were in the air," Patrick said as he put one hand over a red button then continued. "Turbo thruster in three, two, one," he pushed the red button. The spacecraft bolted forward at the speed of sound and continuously grew to over 25,000 miles an hour. "Wooooooooooo," Patrick yelled as he yanked the steering controls causing the aircraft to spin in circles. At that speed, moving the spacecraft was foolish and deadly.

"Knock it off," I managed to say.

Patrick eased off the spinning and put the spacecraft on course. When the target location was locked, Patrick let go of the steering handles. We blasted through the Earth's atmosphere in seconds. The craft began to calm as we entered space.

I looked back to my team. They took the easy way out and used their gas masked to knock them out. Patrick was putting his mask on. I was the only one in the team who would rather wait twenty-two hours then to have a gas knock me out. Patrick fell asleep almost instantly after putting on the mask. I stayed awake and gawked out of the windows into outer space.

I'd been to space many times before, but just staring out into the amazement never got tiring.

Twenty-one hours passed and I had just woken up from a natural sleep, not a gas induced one. The gas was always set to turn off half hour before arriving at the destination. I decided to wake everyone up before then to give us more time to prepare. Slowly, everyone began to wake up. I was already dressed in my space uniform.

They quickly got dressed and began doing a rifle check. Patrick took over the controls and began the landing process. We took our seats as Patrick slowed down the spacecraft. Our estimated time of arrival was in eight minutes.

"Remember," I said, "we're here to see what happened to the communications tower first. If everything looks functional, we move on to the Moonlit Resort. We proceed with caution from there on. There's no telling what we will find, but we always expect the worst. Stick together." The thrusters shut down and we began descending.

I was able to see the communications tower from the sky. Everything looked fine. Nothing looked destroyed or out of place. There were a few new craters around it but that was normal. The moon was always being struck by small meteorites.

"Patrick, take us down near the tower. We'll trek to the hotel when needed," I said.

Patrick took the spacecraft off autopilot and began landing. We hit the surface with a thud. The craft shook as it settled onto the lunar soil. A clear liquid released from the bottom of the spacecraft and sprayed the area around it. The moon's dust likes to stick to things and would likely cause damage to craft, this prevented that from happening.

"Grab your gear," I said as everyone unbuckled.

We grabbed our rifles and masks from the weapons storage container at the craft's rear. The masks strapped around our heads almost like a ski mask. There was a little hose that inserts into our nostrils for air. The hose attaches at the bottom to a small tank, no bigger than a spray paint can. The oxygen in those containers would last twenty-four hours. The masks are equipped with speakers and microphones so we can communicate with each other.

"Let's move out," I said.

The team walked to the door. Patrick pushed the release button. The door hissed and opened exposing the rocky surface of the moon. John, the communications man, jumped out first; followed by Mick, Patrick, Austin and then Orlando. I was the last one out. We quickly got into formation and walked, more like jumped, toward the communications tower. We got to the door and pushed it open. All of us walked inside. I reached for the light switch and pushed it on. The room instantly illuminated with light. John took off his mask and began looking around. The room was large and had a computer system in the center. Surrounding the computer were endless buttons and a few screens. Further into the room was a staircase that led to the top of the antenna tower.

"Marshal," John called out to me. "There's something here you should see."

I walked over to John as he pointed toward the wall. Brown dried blood was smeared across like someone was using it as leverage to walk. I began following the trail. It led up to the tower staircase.

"Two line formation," I ordered. Orlando and Austin took point as Mick and Patrick got behind them. They slowly began to creep up the stairs when we heard it. A loud and sluggish moan blared above us.

"What the fuck was that?" Mick said not able to see what made the noise.

"It sounds like someone's in trouble." Orlando answered.

We heard steps beginning to descend down from the staircase. And soon enough, as the light illuminated the body, we saw it. The image of that man still haunts me till this day. His skin was pale and green. It was missing part of its right cheek revealing teeth and jaw. The man's nose was broken and looked to have been smashed back into his face. Most of its hair was ripped out of its scalp. The monster continued walking down to us as we stared in shock.

"Fall back," I said.

The creature tripped over its feet and tumbled down the remaining steps. It landed face first on the ground making a sickening thud only a foot away from Orlando. We stared at it for a moment, pointing our weapons as it remained motionless. There were gashes on its arm where bone and muscle tissue disgorged out of.

"What is it?" Patrick asked.

"I don't know," I answered. None of us had ever seen anyone who looked like this and still was able to walk.

When I said that, the creature sprang to life. It wrapped its hands around Orlando shin and dragged itself toward him. The beast sank its teeth into Orlando's calf ripping a chunk of clothes and flesh off. He screamed in pain as Austin came to his aid. He pulled the creature from Orlando and shoved him a foot away kicking it across the face. Orlando tried to shift weight from his bitten leg. He lost balance and fell back as blood gushed out of his wound. He continued to scream. We were all dumbfounded at what this cannibalistic person did. I began to shout orders.

"Patrick, take Orlando to the entrance and wrap something around his leg. Everyone else fall back, get away from this thing."

The creature began to rise to its feet. It chewed on the hunk of flesh it bit off of Orlando. Blood gushed out of its mouth and dripped onto the ground as it chewed. Patrick grabbed Orlando by his suit and dragged him to the door. The creature shambled toward us.

I raised my rifle and pulled the trigger. The bullet entered the beast's chest and exploded out of its back. A golf ball size hold appeared where the bullet traveled. It continued walking toward us.

"Fire," I said in shock. No one alive would be able to survive a shot through the chest. Everyone around me raised their weapons and fired. Bullets began to rip through the creature's body; black substance poured out of the open wounds. It fell back and thrashed on the ground. Bullets ricocheted in the room, but luckily no one was struck,

"It's still alive," Austin said in terror as it got back to its feet. The bullet holes all over its body were oozing out black bile.

Mick turned the S-801 rifle scope on. He raised it up to his eyes as best as he could and fired a round through its skull. The impacted caused the top of its scalp to rip open, exposing what was left of its black brain. Mick fired again, this time hitting its center forehead. Brain matter splattered across the wall behind it. The creature fell to the ground smacking what was left of its head on the stairs railing.

Austin turned to tend to his older brother while the rest of us stood in alarm. I shook off my fright and walked toward Orlando. He had a rag tied a little above his knee.

"That's all I could find," Patrick said.

Orlando began to cough up the same black matter as the monster that bit into him. He curled to his side and vomited. Bile was spewing out of his mouth, nose and even his eyes.

"We need to get him back to the ship," I said.

Mick walked up behind me and said, "No, we can't. It looks like that creature over there is infected with something. Orlando has it. He needs to stay here and we should get away from him before we get infected."

Austin was the first to say something, "We're not leaving my brother behind."

The more I thought about the situation, the more I realized that Mick was right. The creature was infected with something. I looked over to John who quickly put his mask back on. Orlando began to convulse on the ground. His skin was turning green and his face was covered in sores.

"Look at him," Mick said. "We need to get out of here."

"No, we're not leaving him." Austin answered.

I looked down at Orlando, he stopped moving. Austin was to busy arguing with Mick to realize what was going on. Orlando's eyes turned black as he stumbled to his feet.

Mick saw him rise and quickly took a few steps back. Austin had his back to him; he slowly turned to look at his brother.

"Orlando?" he said as it lunged for him. Orlando ripped Austin's mask off and bit into his face over his right eye. He sucked the eye out of his socket then chewed. Austin shrieked in pain as he pushed his brother back and covered his wound. Orlando lunged again for him biting into his chin. Mick raised his weapon to his eye and fired. The bullet traveled through Austin's head and exited into Orlando's skull. Both of them crashed to the ground on top of each other as blood and brain matter seeped out of the wounds.

"Sorry, sir," Mick said to me.

I didn't blame him, I actually believed his reasoning. Orlando was bitten and he turned. Austin was bitten and he would have turned. Destroying the brain was the only thing that brought down the first creature.

"No need to be sorry," I added. "You did what you had to." I did feel bad for my two fallen teammates. But I had seen a lot of death. "Listen up," I said to the remaining team. "We need to take their bodies back to the ship. If this is an infection, Zilith will need to study it. All of the communications equipment looks fine. I'm guessing that no one wanted to come in because that thing was here. After we take Orlando and Austin back to the ship we'll head for the resort."

"How are we going to take the bodies? I'm not touching them." Mick asked.

I looked around and saw a roll of plastic wrap in the corner. I grabbed it and began wrapping the dead bodies.

"They look like mummies," Patrick said.

"No jokes, these men use to be our teammates." I said as I grabbed Orlando's body and flung him over my shoulders.

John stood by the door. He nodded and opened it. I walked through the door with him over my shoulder. Patrick and Mick carried Austin behind me. John held his weapon up in case there was another creature lurking in the shadows.

We made it to the ship and put their bodies in the cargo area underneath the craft. John locked the doors and turned to face us.

"Should we call this in?" John asked.

"No," I answered. I didn't want to call anything in until I could confirm what happened to the occupants at Moonlit Resort.

We headed north toward the hotel. From our landing point we could see the structure about a mile away. We trekked with worry and alarm plastered on our faces.

"I can't believe that Austin and Orlando are dead. What the hell was that thing?" John said breaking the silence.

"I don't know," I admitted. "Mick might be right when he said infection. Have you ever read *War of the Worlds*? The Martians thought they could come and take Earth away from us. Despite everything humanity threw at them, it was an infection that ultimately killed off the alien invaders. I think here, we are the aliens and the moon is telling us to leave."

No one spoke after my comment. Maybe they were trying to process what was happening here.

We finally reached the structure. The three-story high hotel was built on a large block of pavement. It was gray and made out of mostly steel. A well-lit green sign that flashed the words; *MOONLIT RESORT was* positioned just above the double doors.

The doors to the building were shut. I took point as I pushed open the first set of doors. Patrick was at the rear, he closed the doors behind him. A robotic voice welcomed us and let us in through the second set of doors. Oxygen began to blow into the room as the last set of doors opened. We held our weapons up as the automatic doors opened.

The lobby was completely decimated. Sofas were overturned.

Broken glass and miscellaneous papers littered the ground. Splatters of blood and pieces of bone and meat were spewed all over the room. I slowly crept into the room. The front desk was to my right. Straight ahead was a large dinning room and to the left were two stair cases and the elevators.

"Hello?" I called out as the lights flickered.

There was no response.

"This is Space Marshal Collins, if anyone is there please respond."

Nothing.

We walked in a square shape formation. First we went through the dining room doors. The lights were off, I flipped the switch next to the door and the florescent lights blinked on. All of the tables and chairs were overturned. Some were broken. Dishes and expired food covered the ground.

"Hello?" I said again, this time a reply came. Several collected moans echoed in the room. Bodies appeared to stand out of nowhere. Before we could blink the room was filled with at least thirty infected, each of them walked toward the open door. They stared at us with vacant and hungry faces. Among the hoard of adults, were a few children as well. They were a little bit fast.

"Fall back," I said. As we turned we saw more of them poring in from the staircase.

Mick raised the gun up his eyes and said, "Marshal, orders?"

I didn't hesitate to yell, "Fire!"

Mick fired four shots into the crowd to bring down the monsters closest to us. John and Patrick began firing wild, un-aimed shots. Surprisingly, they managed to drop a few. We were being cornered by the creatures. Their eyes hungrily stared at us as they advanced; tripping over the creatures we dropped.

We fell back toward the front desk.

"I'm running low," Mick yelled. "We need to find a way out."

As he said that, music began to play from the loud speakers. It was Jazz, something I hadn't heard in years. The creatures stopped moving and stared to the sky. A dumbfounded expression crossed their face. Some sounded like they were humming along with the music. We kept firing, dropping as many near the door as we could.

"We're going to run through them and make it to the door." I said.

Undead Side of the Moon

We managed to make a path and began heading for the door. The music stopped when we were half way there. The creatures stopped staring into the loud speaker and turned too look at us.

I was taking point, Mick was behind me, John and Patrick were close behind. The creatures reach for them. One of them managed to grab hold of Patrick's uniform. He had a few grenades strapped to his belt. The creatures yanked on the belt trying to bring Patrick closer, pulling the pin off one of the grenades. I remember hearing him scream as they swayed him back and forth. A loud beep erupted. The hoard pulled Patrick deeper toward the dining room. He screamed louder as they began tearing him apart. We kept moving toward the door when the grenade exploded. Bodies flew in all directions and the building shook. The blasted caused me to slam up against the door.

I heard a beeping noise and the doors opened. I crawled threw and looked behind me. I couldn't see anyone from my team. All I saw were a few hungry faces staring at me and small patches of fire as the steel doors closed.

Everything else was a blur. I do remember crawling all the way back to the ship as the building burned from the inside. Patrick had everything ready to do. All I had to do was set the autopilot and the craft would do the rest.

When I made it back to Earth, I was instantly quarantined and put into the cell I'm in now. I was interrogated and accused of killing everyone there. I'm sentenced to be hanged until I am dead. They wouldn't listen when I told them what happened at the Moonlit Resort, about the strange lunar infection that killed everyone and turned them into mindless walking corpses. Deep down inside, I have a feeling that the Zilith Corporation knew what was going on and they needed someone to blame. That someone is me.

There was one thing I didn't tell them. When I got back to the ship and took my space suit off, I had these strange scratches on my right shoulder that quickly healed before I landed on Earth. Maybe while I was making my escape one of them scratched me. I'll never know what kind of an effect it'll have on me when I'm dead.

Space Marshal Elroy Collins
January 3rd 2060

About the Authors

R. M. Cochran lives in an undisclosed location in Southern California and writes in his spare time.

Voss Foster lives in a desert town in the middle of Washington State. He has been writing speculative fiction as long as he cares to remember. During the tiny sections of time when he isn't writing, Voss enjoys singing, cooking, playing trombone, photography, and catching up with friends and family. He has also read every book he and his family own at least twice, normally five to twenty times, and always searches for something else to hold his interest.

PATRICK SHAND is a writer of things and stuff. If you were to journey to the future, you would know him as a best-selling novelist and recipient of Sexiest Man of 2014 Award. In the present, however, Patrick scripted a story for IDW Publishing's ANGEL: YEARBOOK, the last volume of their long-running comic book based on Joss Whedon's ANGEL. Patrick also writes/produces plays and teaches screenwriting at Five Towns College. You can read up on his work at http://patrickshand.blogspot.com

R. Phillip Roberts was raised in Ohio on classic horror and science fiction. Having lived in Florida and Louisiana, he currently resides in Illinois. Rumor has it that his heart remains in New Orleans (still beating in a mason jar on a dusty old shelf in the back room of some old crone's voodoo shoppe). With a slanted view of the world (and a Muse by the name of Raven perched upon his shoulder to guide him), he writes horror that blends the supernatural and fantastic with real life atrocities that are instigated by the darker side of man's nature.

Frances Pauli was born and raised in Washington State. She grew up with a love of reading and storytelling, and was introduced to Science Fiction and Fantasy at an early age through the books kept and read by her father. She writes primarily Speculative fiction with touches of Romance, and her work has appeared in both electronic and print formats, anthologies and e-zines. More information about Frances and her stories can be found at: http://francespauli.com

Rebecca Besser, author of "Undead Drive-Thru," is a graduate of the Institute of Children's Literature. Her work has appeared in the Coshocton Tribune, Irish Story Playhouse, Spaceports & Spidersilk, joyful!, Soft Whispers, Illuminata, Common Threads, Golden Visions Magazine, Stories That Lift, Super Teacher Worksheets, Living Dead Presents Magazine, The Broke One, The Stray Branch, and The Undead That Saved Christmas. She also has stories in anthologies by Living Dead Press, Wicked East Press, NorGus Press, Pill Hill Press, Hidden Thoughts Press, Coscom Entertainment, and Knight Watch Press; and a poem in an anthology by Naked Snake Press. Visit her website: www.rebeccabesser.com

James Conway lives in Australia, where he writes fantasy, dystopian, horror and sci-fi. He has been writing since 2008.His biggest influences are, Stephen King and his son Joe Hill, Peter Hamilton and Brandson Sanderson. James loves stories that run with creative style and are as original as one can make them. *The Gift of Innocence, The Tragedy of Ignorance...* is his first published story.

Jason Rodimus Fowler hails from Raleigh, North Carolina, where he began a life-long passion for anything horror related. When he was twelve years old or so his mother handed him a copy of Clive Barker's *The Damnation Game*, and it changed his life forever. J. Rodimus began to write short horror fiction with a flair for dark comedy. His twisted tales of fear and retribution range from battling hordes of the undead, to true love among demon fodder.

Born in 1980, **R. W. Hawkins** is a horror/sci-fi writer who lives in Salisbury, England with his fiancée Sara and their pet dog, Molly. This is his first published work. When he's not writing, he enjoys collecting graphic novels, watching zombie films and thinking about alien invasions and the apocalypse.

Dane T. Hatchell lives in Baton Rouge, LA. He has stories appearing in over fifteen different anthologies from Living Dead Press. You can contact Dane atEnadious@gmail.com

Persephanie Cerda lives in Riverside, California. Embryonic is her first published piece. The story was inspired by her fascination with the human condition; the trials and tribulations that humanity suffers through and an existence which isn't always clear. She would like to thank R. M. Cochran for his words of encouragement and his insatiable urge to edit.

Debate rages over who exactly **Geoffery Crescent** is. Some believe him to be the reincarnation of Phillip Deihl, inventor of the electric ceiling fan. Others think him to be E. F. Summers, a goat farmer from Bavaria. His hobbies include churning butter, melting wax and carving vegetables to look like former US presidents. He is the world expert on soy based meat replacement products. He never completed her Silver Duke of Edinburgh Award and is yet to finish an episode of Deal or No Deal. He has three mothers, but no father, and cannot be killed by conventional means.

John McCuaig was born and raised in Glasgow, Scotland but now lives in London, England. Over twenty of his short stories have been accepted for publication in the past couple of years and his first novel, The Church, was recently released. This year should also see the release of two new novels, for more details of his past, present and future projects please visit his website or blog-johnmccuaig.com and johnmccuaig.blogspot.com

Lyle Perez-Tinics is the creator of www.UndeadintheHead.com a website dedicated to zombie books at the authors. He is the owner and Editor-in-Chief of Rainstorm Press (www.RainstormPress.com) and The Mad Formatter (www.TheMadFormatter.com) a book interior design business. He has stories in many anthologies and is currently working on two novels, *Existing Dead* and *Rising from the Tempest*.

coming soon from
KnightWatch Press

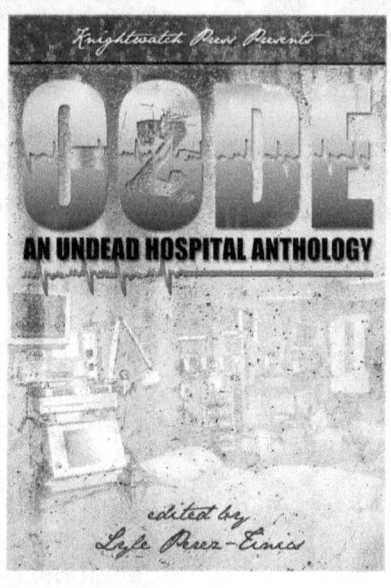

Mark Bliss has spent most of his adult life working at a pawnshop. For years, he has ripped people off with no remorse. That is until the day an elderly woman named Maggie Bliss, walks in through the door and brings an army of living dead with her. DEMENT is a story that truly lives up to its title. Join Mark as he slowly goes insane on the roof of a pawnshop, while the bodies of the dead linger below.

We all know many of the best Zombie flicks and books make their start in or around a hospital but they soon leave the confines of the medical building and start to lay waste to the world but what happens in those first few hours.
" CODE Z - An Undead Hospital Anthology " is a horror anthology with an undead theme. Tales of life excitement and of course the undead. Each story is unique and new.

www.knightwatchpress.info

www.ingramcontent.com/pod-product-compliance
Lightning Source LLC
Chambersburg PA
CBHW070848120626
46556CB00002B/917